"Enter the betrayed wife, with her beautiful chin held high and her sensational green eyes turned to ice. *'I have nothing to say to you, Roque.'*"

He gave a wincingly good mimic of her cool boarding-school accent, bringing an uncomfortable flush to Angie's cheeks.

"I was then treated to the fabulous supermodel walk through the apartment—the long, sexy glide and the sizzling fiery hair—aimed to hook me into following you like a panting puppy dog…"

"A puppy dog?" She was glad to get her teeth into something. "You were never anyone's panting puppy dog, Roque. You came into this world a fully-grown womanizing wolf!"

All about the author...
Michelle Reid

Reading has been an important part of **MICHELLE REID**'s life as far back as she can remember. She was encouraged by her mother, who made the twice-weekly bus trip to the nearest library to keep feeding this particular hunger. In fact, one of Michelle's most abiding memories from those days is coming home from school to find a newly borrowed selection of books stacked on the kitchen table just waiting to be delved into.

There has not been a day since that she hasn't had at least two books lying open somewhere in the house ready to be picked up and continued whenever she has a quiet moment.

Her love of romance fiction has always been strong, though she feels she was quite late in discovering the riches Harlequin Books has to offer. It wasn't long after making this discovery that she made the daring decision to try her hand at writing a Harlequin Presents novel for herself, never expecting it to become such an important part of her life.

Now she shares her time between her large, close, lively family and writing. She lives with her husband in a tiny white stone cottage in the English Lake District. It is both a romantic haven and the perfect base to go walking through some of the most beautiful scenery in England.

Michelle Reid

AFTER THEIR VOWS

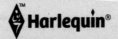

TORONTO NEW YORK LONDON
AMSTERDAM PARIS SYDNEY HAMBURG
STOCKHOLM ATHENS TOKYO MILAN MADRID
PRAGUE WARSAW BUDAPEST AUCKLAND

Recycling programs
for this product may
not exist in your area.

ISBN-13: 978-0-373-13001-6

AFTER THEIR VOWS

First North American Publication 2011

Copyright © 2011 by Michelle Reid

AFTER THEIR VOWS

CHAPTER ONE

'WHAT do you want me to do about it?'

Seated behind his desk, engrossed in the business report spread open in front of him, Roque de Calvhos responded impassively, 'You do nothing.'

Mark Lander continued to hover like a man in a quandary, frowning behind his spectacles because doing nothing was not an option his employer could afford to take.

'She could make trouble,' he dared to offer, all too aware that the younger man did not take kindly to interference into decisions he made about his private life.

Roque de Calvhos was a chip off the old block when it came to a cut-throat mentality. When Eduardo de Calvhos had become ill and died suddenly three years ago, no one had expected his notorious playboy son to calmly stride in here and start making his presence felt, with far-sweeping decisions most people had believed were a precursor to the quick demise of de Calvhos power.

They now knew better. What Roque had done with the huge network of diverse companies which made up the de Calvhos business empire had put his father's colossal success in the shade. Now obsequious respect shadowed the thirty-two-year-old's every elegant footstep. If the financial industry could give out such awards, Roque de Calvhos would have sprouted wings. He was also remarkably good-looking, insufferably laid-back, and so impossible to read that there were still some fools out there who dared to underestimate him—only to learn the hard way what a huge mistake they had made.

His estranged wife was not one of those people. 'At the moment she is citing irreconcilable differences. Think about it, Roque,' Mark advised. 'Angie is basically letting you off the hook here.'

Giving up on the report, Roque sat back in his chair to look up at the older man. Eyes as black as the neatly groomed hair on his head revealed nothing as he studied the lawyer's concerned face.

'You are about to remind me that my wife signed no pre-nup,' Roque predicted. 'Take it from me, Mark, Angie is not greedy. I trust her not to attempt to skin me alive, okay?'

'That depends on what you mean by skinning you alive,' his lawyer responded dryly. 'That she doesn't want your money? Okay, I will agree with you that Angie does not want your money, or she would have been demanding a large cut of it long before now. I would, however, be willing to lay odds that she does not feel the same way about skinning you of your honour and pride. She wants this divorce, Roque.' Mark stated it firmly. 'If the only way she can get it is by playing dirty then you have to consider if you are going to like her citing adultery on your part to get what she wants. If she does decide to go down that route there is just no way we will be able to keep it out of the public arena, and you know as well as I do the old can of worms she will be opening if that happens.'

Roque set his teeth together in frustration behind the moulded shape of his lips because he knew that Mark was right. *The Playboy and the Two Supermodels...* headlines were bound to start up again. Last time, the slick, character-slaying stories had run for weeks, trawling out his cavalier playboy past and quoting phrases about leopards and spots.

He released a sigh, hating it that Mark was right.

Taking that sigh as an indication that he could go on, Mark Lander took in a deep breath and went for broke. 'Angie has hard evidence that you slept with Nadia Sanchez. The stupid woman gave her the evidence herself because she wanted to break up your marriage.'

'She succeeded,' Roque confirmed flatly.

'You were damn lucky back then that Angie decided to keep silent about the affair in an effort to save her own face.'

There was a lot more to Angie's motivations than mere saving face, Roque mused, using the luxuriant swoop of his eyelashes to shade his eyes so that the lawyer could not read his thoughts. Angie was hurting. Angie was nursing the worst kind of broken heart a woman could nurse. Angie blamed him and hated him for causing it.

Angie had also caused a minor sensation when she'd walked away from her modelling career and hadn't been seen again for months. He'd had teams of trackers out looking for her all over Europe without one of them managing to flush her out. He'd hounded her kid brother, hoping that Alex would relent and tell him where Angie was. The then eighteen-year-old had told him nothing and enjoyed watching him suffer. When Angie had eventually turned up again, she'd strolled blithely into CGM Management and asked her old boss Carla for an ordinary office job. Now she fronted the desk at the famous modelling agency, and not once in the whole lousy year of their separation had she acknowledged that he was even alive.

Now she was coming at him with a divorce petition, as if she expected him to jump on it with glee. Roque shaded his eyes by another millimetre, the dark iris glittering calculatingly behind the guard of his eyelashes as he considered the unfinished business he had with his very hurt, very English, runaway wife.

The kind of business which involved Angie crawling on her knees and begging him to take her back. His pride and his badly bruised ego demanded it. And unfortunately for Angie he had the perfect tool with which to make it happen—he was thinking of a matter Mark knew nothing about, which he'd been keeping a close, watchful eye on.

'No divorce,' he announced, making the lawyer start in surprise as he sat forward and returned his attention to the business report.

'So you're just going to ignore it?' Mark said in disbelief.

'I will deal with it,' he promised, 'but in my own time and way.'

Not liking the sound of that, Mark shifted his stance. 'I think it would be—safer to keep this impersonal and go the legal route.'

'"*A esperança é a última que morre,*"' Roque murmured, unaware that he had slipped into his own language until after he'd quoted the old Portuguese proverb with a dryness only he understood.

'Hope is the last one to die,' he translated silently, for no other reason than it felt good to know he had that much faith in Angie coming round to his way of thinking.

Though he had no similar faith in Angie's thieving rat of a kid brother, he tagged on.

After Mark had finally given up on trying to change his mind and left him alone, Roque sat for a few minutes, considering what his next move should be, before he pulled a drawer open in his desk and removed a manila file. A few minutes after that he rang for his car to be brought round to the front of the building, rose up to his full and intimidating six feet three inches of hard muscled height, and strode with his usual casual grace for the door.

'Cambridge,' he instructed his driver, then relaxed back and closed his eyes to contemplate netting a small fish to use as bait to reel in the bigger fish.

The atmosphere in Angie's small kitchen hit strangulation levels. 'You've done *what*?' she choked out in dismay.

Sitting hunched over on a kitchen chair, her brother mumbled 'You heard me.'

Oh, she'd heard him, okay, but that did not mean she wanted to believe what he'd said!

Angie pushed her tumbling mane of fiery hair back from her brow and drew in a breath. When she'd arrived home from work this evening to find Alex already waiting for her, she'd been too pleased to see him to question why he'd made the journey up from Cambridge midweek, with no prior warning that he was planning to pay her a visit. Now she wanted to kick herself for not sensing trouble straight away.

'So, let me just try and get this straight,' she said, fighting to keep her voice level. 'Instead of attending to your studies you've been spending your time gambling on the internet?'

'Playing the stockmarket isn't gambling,' Alex objected.

'What do you call it, then?' Angie challenged.

'Speculating.'

'That's just gambling by another name, Alex!' Angie instantly fired back, 'Stop trying to pretty it up.'

'I wasn't!' he denied. 'Everyone else at uni is doing it! You can make a fortune right now if you know how to play it right.'

'I don't give a damn what everyone else is doing. I only care about you and what you've been doing,' Angie fed back. 'And if you've been making your fortune speculating on the markets, why are you sitting there telling me that you're in debt?'

Like a cornered young stag, her nineteen-year-old brother reared upright. Six feet of long, lanky male, with spiky brown hair and vivid green eyes shot through with burning defence. He threw himself across the room to go and stand glaring out of the window, his hands pushed into the pockets of his zipped-up grey fleece.

The tension in him buzzed. Wrapping her arms around her middle, Angie gave him a minute to get a hold of himself before she pressed quietly, 'I think it's time you told me just how bad it is.'

'You're not going to like it.'

She'd just bet that she wasn't. Angie abhorred debt.

She was *scared* of it. Had been that way from the tender age of seventeen, when their parents had been killed in a car accident, leaving her and her then thirteen-year-old brother to find out the hard way how their privileged lifestyle had been mortgaged to the hilt. What bit was left after probate had finished liquidating their few assets had been barely enough to pay her brother's boarding school fees for the next year. She'd been forced to walk away from her own private education and take two jobs a day in an effort to survive. And she'd worked and scrimped and carefully hoarded every spare penny she'd earned so that she did not fall into debt. If it had not been for a chance meeting with the owner of a top modelling agency she dreaded to think where she and Alex would have ended up.

By then she'd been burning both ends of the candle for twelve long, miserable months, serving behind one of the beauty counters in a London department store by day, and serving tables in a busy City restaurant by night, before going home to her miserable bedsit to sleep like one exhausted and then getting up to repeat the same routine again the next day.

Then Carla Gail happened to come to her counter to buy perfume. Carla had spotted something marketable in Angie's reed-thin figure—exaggerated in those days because she hadn't been getting enough to eat—her emerald-green eyes, and the bright auburn hair set against her dramatically pale skin. Without really knowing how it had happened she'd found herself propelled into the unnatural world of high fashion, earning the kind of money that could still catch her breath when she thought about it.

Within months she was the model everyone wanted

on their catwalk or on the front cover of their magazines. She'd spent the next three years following the fashion drum around the world. She'd stood for hours while designers fitted their creations to her long slender figure, or posed in front of cameras for glossy fashion shoots—and she had willingly accepted every single second of it, coveting the money she earned so she could keep Alex safe in his boarding school environment.

Her proudest achievement, in Angie's view, had been ensuring that Alex never missed out on a single thing his more privileged schoolfriends enjoyed doing. When he'd won a place at Cambridge she'd felt as pleased and as proud as any parent could, and she'd done it all without once being tempted to take on debt.

'It's all right for you.' Her brother broke into her reverie. 'You're used to having money to play with, but I've never had any for myself.'

'I give you an allowance, Alex, and I've never denied you a single thing you've asked for over and above that!'

'It was the asking that stuck in my throat.'

Tightening her arms across her body in an effort to crush the pangs of hurt she experienced at that totally unfair response, it took Angie a few seconds before she could dare let herself speak.

'Come on,' she urged heavily then. 'Just get it over with and spit out how much it is we're discussing, here.'

With a growling husk of reluctance Alex quoted a figure which blanched the colour out of Angie's face.

'You're joking,' she whispered.

'I wish.' He laughed thickly.

'Fifty—did you just say *fifty* thousand?'

Turning around, Alex flushed. 'You don't have to beat me over the head with it.'

Oh, but she did! 'How the heck did you get the credit to spend *fifty* thousand on speculation, for goodness' sake?'

Silence came charging back at her as they stood with the width of the kitchen between them, Angie taut as a bowstring now, with her arms rod-straight at her sides, and her brother with his chin resting on his chest.

'Answer me, Alex,' she breathed unsteadily.

'Roque,' he growled.

Roque—?

For a horrible second Angie felt so light-headed she thought she was actually going to faint. She tried for a breath and didn't quite make it. 'Are—are you telling me that—*Roque* has been encouraging you to play the stockmarkets?'

'Of course he hasn't!' her brother flung back in disgust. 'I wouldn't take his advice if he did. I hate him—you know that. After what he did to you, I—'

'Then what are you saying?' Angie sliced through what he wanted to say, 'Because I'm really confused here as to why you've even brought his name into this!'

Alex scuffed a floor tile with a trainer-shod foot. 'I used one of your credit cards.'

'But I don't use credit cards!'

She had the usual cash debit cards everyone needed to survive these days, but never, ever had Angie dared to own a credit card—because a credit card tempted you to go into debt, and debt was...

'The one that Roque gave to you.'

Angie blinked. The one that Roque gave to her... The credit card attached to Roque's bottomless financial resources that she had never used, though the card still languished in this apartment somewhere, like a—

'I came across it in your bedside drawer last time I was here and...'

She sucked in a painfully sharp breath. 'You went through my private things?'

'Oh, hell,' her brother groaned, shifting his long body in a squirm of regret. 'I'm sorry!' he cried. 'I don't know what came over me! I just—needed some money, and I didn't want to have to ask you for it, so I went looking to see if you'd any spare cash hanging around the flat. I saw the card lying there in your bedside drawer, and before I knew what I was doing I'd picked it up! It had *his* fancy name splashed all over it—the great and glorious *De Calvhos Bank*!' he rasped out, revealing the depth of his dislike for a man he had never tried to get along with. 'At first I meant to cut it into little pieces and post them back to him with a – message. Then I thought, why not see if I can use it to hit him where it will hurt him the most? It was really easy...'

Angie stopped listening at *easy*. She was so sure that she was going to really faint away this time that she reached for a chair and sat down on it, lifting up a set of icy fingers to cover her trembling mouth.

Roque—dear God. Closing her eyes, she gave a helpless shake of her head. 'I don't want to believe you could do this to me,' she whispered against her cold fingers.

'What do you want me to say?' her brother choked out. 'I did a stupid thing, and now I'm sorry I did— but he was supposed to take care of you, Angie! You *deserved* to be taken care of for a change. Instead he cheated on you with Nadia Sanchez and—well, now look at you.'

She flicked her startled eyes open, 'Wh-what's wrong with me?'

Alex let loose with a short laugh, as if she'd made a stupid joke. 'You used to have the kind of career most girls only dream about, Angie. I couldn't look around without seeing you plastered on a billboard or a magazine somewhere. You were famous—fabulous. My friends used to envy me for having such a gorgeous sister. They'd fight each other for a chance to meet you. Then Roque came along turned you inside out. You stopped modelling because *Roque didn't like it*—'

'That's not true—'

'Yes, it is!' His face was hot with anger now. 'He was a selfish, arrogant, superior swine who wanted to rule over you like a tyrant. He didn't like your job commitments—your commitment to *me*.'

There was a bit too much truth in that part for Angie to argue with it. Roque *had* demanded her exclusive attention. In fact Roque had been demanding all round— her attention, first call on her loyalty, the full extent of her desire for him focused on him between the sheets...

'Now you work at a lousy reception job for the same modelling agency that used to roll out the red carpet every time you walked into it. And you struggle to make ends meet again while *he* flies the world in his private jet, and I daren't ask you for an extra penny any more without feeling as guilty as sin. Roque owed me big-time for what he did to you, Angie, and you just let him get away with it—as if—'

'He owes *me*, not you!' Angie flared in response to all of that. 'Roque was *my* mistake, not your mistake, Alex. He never did a single thing to you!'

'Are you kidding?' her brother flared back. 'He robbed me of the sister I used to be proud of and left me with the empty shell I'm looking at now! Where's your natural vibrancy gone, Angie? Your stylish sparkle? *He* took them.' He answered his own bitter question. 'If Roque had not married you and then cheated on you, you would not be floating through life looking like the stuffing has been knocked out of you. You would still be flying way up there at the top of your profession, raking in the money, and I would not have needed to use his credit card to play the markets because *you* would have financed me!'

Of everything he had just thrown at her in that last bitter flood, the part making its biggest impact on Angie was seeing the truth about the brother she so totally adored staring her hard in the face. In her endless efforts to make his life as comfortable as she could possibly make it for him she had created a monster. A bone-selfish, petulant man-child who thought it was okay to steal someone else's money if it got him what he wanted.

What was it Roque had said during one of their fights about her brother? 'You are in danger of creating a life-wasting lout if you don't stop it.'

Well, that damning prediction had come true with a vengeance, Angie saw—only to toss that aside again with a stubborn shake of her head. For what gave Roque the right to criticise the way she'd handled a rebellious teenager when his own privileged upbringing had given him everything he wanted at the nod of his handsome dark head?

Alex had been only seventeen when she'd first met Roque, still attending boarding school and reliant on her for everything. Falling in love had not been an option she could afford to let happen—yet she'd been unable to stop herself from falling for Roque. And what Roque wanted Roque got, by sheer single-minded force of will—which in Angie's view put him and Alex in the same selfish club. Between the two of them they had demanded so much from her that sometimes she'd felt stretched so taut in two different directions she'd thought she might actually snap in two.

On one side of her she'd had the brother who'd become such a handful to deal with, skipping lessons to go out on the town with his friends and constantly getting into scrapes, which meant she'd had to travel down to his school in Hampshire to deal with the inevitable fall-out. Then there'd been Roque on the other side, angry with her for pandering to her brother's every whim.

But at least she'd felt vindicated when Alex won a place at Cambridge. He hadn't achieved that by spending every night out on the town. And he'd settled into university life over the last year without giving her very much grief.

Then she shook her head—because Alex *hadn't* settled down at all, had he? He'd just hidden it from her that he was still doing exactly what he wanted to do—even if that meant sneaking around her flat and stealing credit cards to pay for his excesses.

'I hate him,' Alex said, with no idea what his sister was thinking. 'It would've served him right if I'd gone on a real bender and completely cleaned him out. I should've bought a yacht or two, or a private plane like his to fly myself around in, instead of sitting in my room

at uni spending his rotten money before he found out it
was me doing the—'

Alex snapped his mouth shut, leaving the rest of what
he had been going to say to slam around the room like
a clap of thunder.

Angie shot to her feet.

'Finish that,' she shook out.

Biting out a curse, her brother lifted a hand and
grabbed the back of his neck. 'Roque came to see me
on campus today,' he confessed. 'He called me a weak,
thieving wimp and threatened to break my neck if I
didn't—' He stopped, clearly deciding to swallow down
the rest of the insults Roque must have thrown at him.
'The bottom line is,' he went on huskily, 'he wants his
money back, and he told me that if I don't give it to him
he's going to take the matter to the police.'

The police—? Angie sat down again.

'Now I'm scared, because I don't think he was bluff-
ing. In fact I know that he wasn't.'

So did Angie. Roque did not make threats unless he
was prepared to carry them through—as she'd discovered in the hardest way there was.

Bitterness suddenly grabbed at her insides, burning
a hole in her ability to hold back from recalling that
final showdown, when she and Roque had stood toe to
toe like mortal enemies instead of loving husband and
wife.

*'I am warning you, Angie, go chasing off to your
brother's aid this time and I will find someone else to
take your place tonight.'*

She'd gone. He'd found Nadia. Marriage over.

Pulling back from where those memories wanted to
suck her, Angie sat back in the chair. 'So, how does he

expect you to pay him back?' she asked heavily, already suspecting what was coming before her brother loped over to the table and produced something from the back pocket of his jeans.

'He said to give you this…'

He was holding out a business card, which he set down on the table in front of Angie. Looking down at it, she saw '*Roque Agostinho de Calvhos*,' printed in elegant black script below the de Calvhos family crest, which crowned just about everything in Roque's world—from his high-end international investment empire to some of the finest vineyards in his native Portugal and vast tracts of inherited land in Brazil.

'He wrote something on the back,' her brother indicated awkwardly.

Reaching out, Angie flipped the card over with a set of ice-cold fingers. '*Eight o'clock. The apartment. Don't be late,*' Roque had scrawled there.

If she'd had it in her Angie would have scratched out a dry, mocking laugh.

The underscored *don't* was the ultimate command from a man who'd grown very intimate with her most besetting sin—an innate lack of good time-keeping. She'd kept him waiting at airports and restaurants. She'd kept him kicking his heels in their apartment while she rushed around like a headless chicken, getting ready to go out. She caught a sudden sharp glimpse of him waiting for her, looking tall, dark and fabulously turned out for a night at the theatre, lounging stretched out in a chair with his eyes closed, his silky black eyelashes resting against his high-sculpted cheekbones, his wide, full and sensual mouth wearing the look of long-suffering patience he could pull off with such excruciating effect.

He'd lost all patience with her, and perhaps she'd deserved it, Angie acknowledged—but enough to send him into the arms of another woman?

And not just any woman, his *ex* woman.

'Will you go and see him?'

Having to blink to bring herself back from where she had gone off to, Angie swallowed thickly and gave a nod of her head.

'Thanks.' Her brother heaved in a long breath. 'I knew you wouldn't let me down.'

So did Roque, thought Angie.

'Look…' Alex shuffled his feet. 'It's already seven o'clock, so I'll go now, sh-shall I? So you can—get ready…'

Desperate to escape now he'd done what he'd come here to do, Alex was already heading for the door when Angie stopped him.

'The credit card?' she prompted. 'Where is it?'

She watched his shoulders give a wincing twitch. 'Roque took it.'

'Good,' Angie murmured, and watched him flinch again as her meaning struck home.

Alex now knew he had lost her trust in him. Her home had always been his home—he had his own bedroom here, his own key. He'd had the same things at the apartment she'd shared with Roque. He was family. You should be able to trust family.

As if he knew what she was thinking, Alex twisted round to aim her a glancing look of remorse. 'I really—really am sorry, Angie,' he husked out painfully. 'I'm sorry for all of it—but especially for dropping this part on to you.'

He'd done that because he had no other option. He'd

done it because she'd always been there to fight his battles for him.

'I promise you on my life I won't ever do anything like this again.'

Looking up at him, Angie saw their father's hair and nose and their mother's eyes and mouth. The aching urge to just get up and go over there to hug him, reassure him that everything was going to be okay, almost got the better of her. But for the first time since she'd taken responsibility for him she controlled the urge.

'I'll call you later,' was all she said, and after a few more seconds of helpless hovering he turned and slunk away, leaving her alone with Roque's business card and that oh-so brief message to stare at.

Eight o'clock. The apartment. Don't be late.

Angie felt a pang of wry appreciation for his slick, short way of getting his message across. She wasn't a fool. She knew the divorce papers would have landed on Mark Lander's desk today, and this was Roque's response to them—with her brother sent along to deliver it and add a bit of clout.

A lot of clout, she extended.

Eight o'clock. The apartment. Don't be late...

Angie drew in a deep, fortifying breath. Well, she could do that, she told herself, aware that she really didn't have a choice. However, she would not be turning up in the role of a wimpy victim Roque was expecting to see, she determined grimly as she rose to her feet. Her brother might see her as a pathetic creature with all the stuffing knocked out of her, but she was not and would never be that feeble! She'd spent too many years fighting her own battles to let fear of what Roque could do to Alex grind her to a quivering pulp now.

On that bracing reminder, Angie tossed her hair back over her narrow shoulders and stepped across the kitchen to catch up her bag. A minute later she was standing in her hall, dragging on her coat as she followed her brother out of the door.

CHAPTER TWO

FRESH from the shower, Roque took a call from the lobby informing him that his wife had arrived in the building with a flicker of surprise.

She was half an hour early.

A deliberate ploy on her part aimed to back-foot him, or was she just running scared? he mused curiously as he rubbed his wet hair with a towel. He was under no illusion that she had rushed over here because she was eager to see him. Only two things fired up Angie enough to make her expose any hint of weakness like this—her brother and money.

If he left out the other thing she always fired up for, which was him. His hands and his mouth on her body, her complete lack of self-control when it came to the pleasure he could inflict on her smooth silken flesh. She knew it too, which was why she had spent the last twelve months avoiding all contact with him.

Or it was one of the reasons, he amended with a frown as he strode into his dressing room and came out again a minute later, still flipping shut the last few buttons on a pale blue shirt across the deeply tanned contours of his taut stomach.

He heard the warning ping telling him that the lift

was arriving as he put a comb through his still damp hair. He headed out of the bedroom onto the elegant spread of the mezzanine landing which looked down on the spacious luxury of open-plan living backed by panoramic views of London's skyline and his long, graceful stride took him down the stairway and across an expanse of rich dark teak wood flooring to the squared opening that led to the inner foyer which housed his private lift.

His confidence that he had Angie exactly where he wanted her was absolute. He did not even question that belief. Angie might prefer to run in the opposite direction but she could not, because the chains of loyalty to her brother were too heavy and too tight. In a few seconds she was going to step out of the lift into his waiting clutches, having dragged herself and those chains across London to get here. An hour after that she would be back in his bed, where she belonged, chains and all, he promised himself.

With that very satisfying moment to look forward to, Roque propped a shoulder up against the wall beside him, slid his hands into the pockets of his black silk trousers and watched as the lift doors slid open, revealing to him the wife he had not set eyes on in almost a year.

Slender and tall, dressed from neck to feet in dramatically unrelieved black, with her flame-bright hair spun in fiery tendrils around her once famous, extraordinarily beautiful, green-eyed, passionate-mouthed face.

Sensation shot across the gap towards him, generated by the highly charged mix of burning acrimony, icy defensiveness and a transparent spark of sexual alertness that hit Roque with a hot stab of tingling provocation low down in his pelvis.

Angie just froze for a second, momentarily stunned by the shock of actually looking at him in the flesh.

She had spent the time it had taken the lift to bring her up twenty floors of luxury living charging up her defences in preparation for this moment, but as she stood staring across the gap separating them she was discovering she had no control whatsoever over the sudden accelerated punch of her heartbeat or the aching thickness that had taken a stranglehold on her throat.

And she knew the reason why she was suffering like this. For almost twelve long months she'd blocked Roque out as if he wasn't a real person. If she'd thought about him at all it had been from within a thick fog. She was good at blocking out things she did not want to look at—had been doing it for most of her adult life. But this was bad, she recognised as her breathing stalled altogether. She had to fight hard to stop her feelings from showing on her face. She'd expected to feel nothing. She'd wanted him to leave her cold. It was almost grotesque to discover that far from feeling nothing she was feeling everything. The old fierce, unstoppable attraction, the sexual excitement stirring up her blood. Even the desperate, aching clutch of hurt was a feeling. It just wasn't fair.

He was so tall he was intimidating, and that was saying something when she was no small thing herself. And the way he was standing across the lobby, backed by warm accent colours of brick-red and aubergine, framed by the soft lighting, he could have easily passed for a brooding, dark male model posing for a glossy photo shoot. His raven-black hair was wearing a luxurious damp sheen to it, and the smooth gloss of his olive-toned skin highlighted the kind of cheekbones any male model would pay with their souls to possess.

As if someone was working her by remote control, she just couldn't stop her eyes from drifting down his supremely elegant stance. His wide shoulders and long, powerful torso were encased in fine pale blue shirting, the top two buttons left undone to reveal a tantalising hint of the warm brown skin lurking beneath. Her mouth ran dry as she looked at that dark golden triangle. She tried not to give in and moisten her lips with the tip of her tongue. Dragging her gaze lower, she saw his hands were lost inside the silk lined pockets of his smooth black trousers—trousers that lovingly skimmed his taut narrow hips and his long, long powerful legs.

As her senses came alive like crazed vandals she knew what she was experiencing was all her own stupid fault.

She should not have blocked him out so thoroughly. Familiarity bred contempt. She should have made herself remember him in fine detail at least twice a day. She should have listed his assets—and he had a lot of them—then eventually she would have started finding a million faults. She'd witnessed this happen so many times in her line of business. One day you were right up there with the best of them, the next you'd suddenly grown a bigger nose, or your smile was no longer as alluring as they'd thought it was and your legs were too fat.

So where did she look to hunt down Roque's physical faults? she asked herself.

'Well, is everything still where it should be?'

The soft, slightly husky accented prompt brought

her eyes flickering back to his face. His half-hidden eyes were as black as midnight; a half-smile curved his wide, passionate mouth. The same half-smile she had been drawn towards from the first time she'd looked at him. The same hot, breathless sensation filled her now as powerfully as it had done back then.

Only this time it hurt to feel like that. This time she saw that beautiful mouth giving pleasure to another woman's mouth. She saw those deep, dark long-lashed eyes warming for someone else.

Roque watched as she stiffened up like a slender column of concrete. He watched the darkened shimmer in her beautiful eyes fade to hurt, then chill to ice.

Something grabbed hold of his loins like a strongly clenched fist and anger flared deep in his chest. He wanted to go over there and grab hold of her by her tension-packed narrow shoulders and give her a damn good shake.

As if she knew what he was thinking defiance sparked—always that sharp, stinging sizzle of defiance came shooting back at him from this woman, if they were in the middle of a fight or making love. He watched her cute, almost pointed chin lift upwards, the way she pinched in the delicate corners of the beautiful mouth. Even the way she tossed her head back, sending the glorious weight of loose silky red spirals trembling back from her face, was a form of defiance.

'I have absolutely nothing to say to you, Roque,' she told him.

Roque allowed his lips to twist out a mocking smile, 'No, I could sense that talking was not in your mind when you looked me over, *meu querida.*'

Annoyed with herself for giving him the weapons to

fire off that taunting shot, Angie stepped out of the lift and into the lobby, which fed all those extra services this vast-sized apartment enjoyed—like the full-size swimming pool and the all-purpose gym, the glass-covered garden that had always reminded her of an exotic hothouse where she'd once done a shoot at Kew.

Angie walked towards him, glazing him out of focus and determined to keep him like that. He did not move a single muscle as she approached. Angie gauged the gap in the arch to one side of him to make sure she had enough room to pass through it without needing him to move out of her path.

She knew exactly where she was heading, so she made the long lines of dark teak flooring her runway. It was like falling off a bike, she discovered. Once you got back on the rest came naturally—even down to blocking her audience out.

Roque followed the long graceful glide of her body as she walked towards him. He knew what she was doing. He'd been handed this kind of treatment before. Angie could be irritatingly focused when she wanted to be, infuriatingly stubborn and tough. Once he had dared to believe he was marrying a sweet and innocently naive lost creature. A lonely child trapped inside a woman's body because she'd never given herself the chance to properly grow up and taste life. He'd soon learnt that the stubborn child in Angie had a grip of steel. The simple truth of it was she didn't want to be anything other than what she was.

Except in his bed, he reminded himself. In his bed, in his arms, she lost the will to fight him on every level—and so fast it was like watching driftwood catching light.

On that grim reminder as to where he intended this evening to end up, Roque allowed his gaze to drift over her again. She was wearing a short black raincoat, tightly cinched to her waist, and her amazing long legs were sheathed in matt black. She had on a pair of flat black ballet shoes that did nothing to diminish her elegant height, and a bright green bag he had not noticed before swung from one shoulder—one of those extravagantly sized bags that were the fashion right now, which she kept crushed to her side with a taut elbow as she walked.

The temptation to reach out and take it from her as she levelled with him curled his fingers into a light fist. The urge to pull her to a stop by placing his hands on her shoulders and then spin her around to make her acknowledge him properly stung like an itch he could not scratch. But he was curious as to what she thought she was up to, arriving early and then just walking past him as if she was the one of them in control here.

So, instead of spoiling her frankly impressive entrance, he turned to follow in her wake.

Angie cut a weaving line through the different cleverly designed living areas. She did not glance at the fabulous view to be enjoyed through the wall-to-wall windows. She did not glance up at the mezzanine gallery where the bedroom suites were situated. She was heading for the only room down here to have a solid door guarding it.

Roque's study.

Her soft mouth set like a clamp as she turned the handle and pushed the door open, then felt an aching squeeze of emotion challenge her composure as she took the first step into what she'd always thought of as his domain.

Everything in this room was as tastefully designed as the rest of this vast place, but in here was Roque's personal stamp. A telltale glimpse at the deeply serious side to his complex personality displayed in the rows of lovingly collected first edition books lining the rows of shelving, and the heavy black leather recliner on which he liked to stretch out to read.

The only television set in the whole apartment rested wafer-thin and flat against a wall of burnt orange. Beneath it spread all the technology required to make it and his complex music system feed sound throughout the whole apartment. Then, of course, the usual computer and communication equipment had a place, as you would expect of a man as internationally structured as him.

But the desk—the big, hand-carved antique desk made of rich dark colonial rosewood he'd had shipped here from his family estate—stood dead centre of everything, making a major statement about his proud Portuguese roots. He could spend hours sitting at that desk, working with a concentration Angie had used to find unfathomably sexy. The cut of his wide shoulders as he leant forward, the sheen of light across his bent head, and his strong, handsome features etched by a depth of concentration that she...

Angie sucked in a breath, not wanting to go there. Not wanting to recall anything intimate about their time spent here together or the fact that there were times when they'd actually existed here in peace.

Yet, right on the back of that desire not to remember, she saw herself, curled up in his recliner with her cheek

supported on a cushion she'd filched from a living room
sofa, slender white fingers idly twirling a ringlet of hair
while she read one of her own meagre assortment of
books.

Contentment… Her throat began to hurt. Bare pink
toes curling and uncurling in time with the music playing softly in the background. A glass of wine and a snack
within lazy reaching distance and her handsome dark
man pooled in the desk light only a couple of metres
away.

Her eyes dared to glaze with moisture for a second.
Then she winked it away, drew in a breath, and made
herself walk over to the desk.

She heard Roque pause in the doorway. The silence
between them buzzed. He was curious, she knew that,
waiting to discover what had brought her in here before
he made any kind of comment.

But that was Roque—a master of strategic timing,
Angie thought dryly as she set her bag down on the top
of his desk, then began rummaging inside its capacious
depths with a frowning ferocity that helped to keep her
focused.

'Okay, I will bite,' he drawled lazily. 'What are you
doing?'

'You should have known to lay off my brother,' Angie
responded. 'You know you don't have a single leg to
stand on by threatening him with the police, because
that credit card was mine.'

'Linked to my personal bank account,' he confirmed,
moving closer.

'Then you only have yourself to blame if you don't
like what I did with it. A wiser man would have can-
celled it the same day I walked out.'

'Strange,' Roque said, 'but I had this rather touching image of you cutting it into little pieces and then depositing the bits—ceremonially, of course—into some fiery hot furnace.'

Angie paused over what she was doing to wonder why she hadn't thought of doing exactly that, instead of shutting the card away in a drawer.

'Well, I didn't,' she said, 'and now you know why I didn't.'

He arrived at her side to settle the lean cut of his hips against the edge of the desk. 'Are you telling me that you gave your brother permission to squander my money?'

Refusing to so much as glance at him, Angie returned to hunting through the assortment of things she kept in her bag while she fought a fierce battle with herself over giving him the honest answer or—

'Yes,' she forced out.

'Liar.' He sighed in disappointment. 'We both know that you would rather pluck out your fingernails than hand over a credit card to your greedy brother.' Reaching up, he gently brushed a twisting length of hair back from her smooth cheek. 'You are one of those rare creations—an honest person, Angie,' he murmured, grimacing when she flinched away from his touch. 'I recall a time when you even made me drive you back into the centre of Lisbon because some shop assistant had overpaid you ten euros in your change. How many people do you think bother to do that, *meu querida*? Even honest people?'

Fingers closing around her chequebook, Angie drew it out of her bag, 'You move in the wrong circles,' she countered. 'You want to try working in a shop—then you would know how that poor assistant would have had to make up the shortfall from her own purse if I hadn't made the effort to take it back.'

'However, as you informed me at the time, I am too rich to know how the real world works.'

'Look…' She turned her face to spear him a fierce look. 'I was the one that played the stockmarkets, okay?'

Eyes of a disturbingly fathomless black held hers steady. 'That makes it two lies you've told me.'

Angie tugged in a breath. 'I decided it was time I made you pay for the months of hell I endured being your stupid blind wife.'

'Blind?' he echoed musingly, indecently long eyelashes lowering slightly. 'Mmm,' he confirmed, 'very blind.'

Angie looked away from him, feeling hot suddenly, and agitated when she'd been so determined to feel nothing at all. Pushing her bag to one side, she spied Roque's fountain pen lying on his blotter and reached for it. Aware that he was watching her every move, she opened the chequebook and bent over it to write.

What happened next threw her totally. In her own way she had been so fixed on what she intended to do that she had not given a thought as to how Roque might react. So his hand suddenly arriving to grasp her wrist, long brown fingers closing like a clamp and then tightening their grip, surprised her into uttering a sharp squeaking gasp.

'Drop the pen,' he gritted.

Angie's fingers tightened in direct objection to his command. 'I was just—'

'I know what you were doing,' he cut in thinly. 'And I, as you see, am stopping you. So drop the pen, Angie.'

When she still refused to comply, the air left his lungs on a hiss. In a smooth snaking move he had completely surrounded her with his hard body as he rose up to swing in behind her, his other hand reaching out to snatch the pen from her, then tossing it away in contempt across the desk.

'Y-you—'

'Shut up,' he growled.

Still holding her wrist imprisoned, he picked up her chequebook next, so he could read what she'd managed to write. Another hiss of anger shot from him, making Angie quiver, because his warm breath had seared across her already burning cheek.

She gave a yank of her wrist and managed to free it, then spun around to glare at him. 'I'm not into cavemen!'

'My apologies.' He took a step back.

Her heart was thumping heavily and her breathing was clipped short. There was a terrible quiver going on inside her and— 'Then what was all that about?' she shook out.

Roque was still frowning at her hurried scribble, all hint of lazy humour wiped clean from his face. He threw out a few tart lucid curses, tossed the chequebook back down on the desk, then spun on his heel to pace away from her like a big prowling cat spoiling for a good fight.

Jerking up her hand to rub at her wrist where it still burned and tingled, Angie watched him warily, still feeling shaken and really uncertain of her ground now—

because she had seen Roque angry before but never like this.

'Twenty damn thousand,' she heard him mutter, as if the sum was an insult.

'It's all I have right now!' she cried out. 'I mean to pay you the rest when—when I can. I just need—'

'It is not your debt, Angie!' He swung round on her forcefully.

Green eyes shimmered, 'What does it matter to you so long as you get your money back?'

Roque scowled, his black satin eyebrows fusing together across the bridge of his long, thin flaring nose. 'I did not allow for this,' he muttered.

'Allow for what?' Angie demanded in bewilderment. 'That I might still have some money of my own left?'

'And this is it?' The look he seared her brought her lips together with a tingling tremor of a snap. 'Twenty lousy thousand is all you have left from your modelling days? Where has the rest gone, Angie?' He strode back towards her in a way that sent her sinking backwards against the desk, but all he did was stop in front of her. 'You were earning big money when I met you. The kind of money even your high-maintenance brother could not spend, given the chance.'

Angie moved a narrow shoulder. 'I b-bought my f-flat—'

'Cash?' he fired at her.

Having found her dry lips had stuck together, Angie nodded.

'Cash…' Roque made a sound of disgust. 'Only you would hand over that amount of money in *cash*!'

'At least I did not go into debt, like most people do.' She defended her strict principles.

Like a man unsure what he wanted to do next, Roque swung away again—only to swing straight back, catching Angie out so that she blinked.

'No, you don't have a clue what it is like to go into debt, do you? Which is why you believed you could stroll in here like a holier-than-thou prima donna and calmly hand me an instalment on your stupid brother's debt and it would make everything all right!'

'I am not playing the prima donna!' Angie protested.

His expressive eyebrows rose to a sardonic arch. 'Enter the betrayed wife, with her beautiful chin held up high and her sensational green eyes turned to ice. "*I have nothing to say to you, Roque.*"' He gave a wincingly good mimic of her cool boarding school accent, bringing an uncomfortable flush to Angie's cheeks. 'I was then treated to that fabulous supermodel walk through the apartment, the long sexy glide and the sizzling fire hair aimed to hook me into following you like a panting puppy dog—'

'A puppy dog?' She was glad to get her teeth into something. 'You were never anyone's panting puppy dog, Roque. You came into this world a fully grown, womanising wolf!'

In a totally unexpected turn of mood, a shaft of pure amusement spread across his face, and he bared his perfectly even flashing white teeth, then uttered a low, sexy growl in response.

Angie received that growl with a burst of indignant fury which set her eyes sparking and her slender body tensing away from the desk.

The sting Roque felt hit his loins was hot. She was going to launch a physical attack on him. He could read her like an open book. When he flipped the mood over between them like this she never could resist rising to the bait. Every muscle he possessed went on alert, ready to catch her when she attacked. The inside of his mouth moistened in anticipation, his lips filling with warm pulsing blood.

He watched her take a step towards him, sensational in anger, so beautiful to look at, and so much his woman he—

Then he saw her remember, watched her eyes darken and her flushed cheeks wash white. In an abrupt movement she spun back round to face the desk again.

Disappointment grabbed at every alerted instinct inside him and closed them all down into a single tight clench. Once, just once, he had called her bluff when she'd firmly put her brother between them. If he'd ever wondered what it was like to stumble into a deep black hole of his own damn making then he'd found out that long and miserable night.

Anger and guilt rolled around Roque's chest in equal measures, followed by a bitterness that thankfully over-shadowed the other two feelings—because the devil if he was going to apologise, he told himself harshly. The devil if he was going to explain himself or the motives of that foolish bitch Nadia now, when it was twelve months too late.

And this was about Angie's brother, he reminded himself grimly. Alex—the spoiled, weak, thieving lout.

Stubborn to the last drop of her hot swirling blood, Angie opened up the chequebook, then stretched across the desk to recover the pen. With a firm scrawl she laid her signature in the appropriate place.

Angelina de Calvhos... She stared at it, vowing fiercely that it was going to be the very last time she would *ever* sign that name.

Then he was right there behind her again like some grim dark power force, reaching for the chequebook again, taking it from her resistant fingers yet again. This time he took it with him as he strode around the desk. With a finality that made Angie choke out a gasp, he opened a drawer and dropped the book into it, then closed the drawer again with a resolute snap.

Tall, dark, supremely in control of himself, he then lifted his proud dark head. 'I think we will begin this again from a more formal perspective,' he intoned coolly.

Angie snapped her arms across her body to contain the way it wanted to shiver in the sudden chill. 'Please don't hurt my brother,' she begged.

CHAPTER THREE

LIKE a man hewn from stone, Roque showed no reaction whatsoever to her quivering climb-down.

'He is a thief.' He stated it brutally. 'He stole your identity and committed credit card theft! And he did it with a complete disregard to the amount of money he was stealing from me. How can you, Angie, of all people, want to defend him for doing that?'

She'd winced all the way through his cold judgement of Alex, but still it did not change a thing she felt. 'He's my brother,' she whispered.

And there it was, Roque recognised, the unconditional love she had a right to expect her brother to return in equal measures. But somehow she did not seem to understand that.

'I can pay you back the full amount he st…spent,' she insisted, with only that small but telling fault in the middle. 'I will just need a little time to get it.'

'By selling your flat and making yourself homeless?' Roque was not impressed.

Neither was Angie. She flared him a scornful look, 'My flat is worth more than fifty thousand pounds, Roque,' she informed him. 'And you already have twenty thousand sitting in that chequebook you've just stolen from me and put in that drawer!'

Fifty… Roque had stopped listening at *fifty*. His lean face carefully without expression, he added *lying wimp* to his brother-in-law's steadily mounting list of sins.

'I'll—I'll go back to modelling,' she explained quickly. 'I'm still in demand, and Carla keeps on trying to get me to change my mind, so I could earn the rest in—in—'

The way Roque flung himself across to the plate glass window behind the desk and thrust his hands in his pockets made Angie's voice slither to a strangled stop. It wasn't so much that he'd turned his back on what she'd been saying but the way he had done it which filled her with dread.

When he wanted to, Roque could become chillingly unreachable. And he felt no love for Alex at all. In his view her brother was the main reason why their marriage had fallen apart. He'd refused to understand that in taking on the parental mantle for her brother she had a duty to see her responsibilities to Alex through—even when they intruded an awful lot on their marriage.

It was just the way things had to be. Teenagers by reputation were rebellious and pushy and difficult. And, okay, so Alex had played up to Roque's often stinging criticism of him, she conceded, but even that did not change the unalterable fact that standing between the two of them had made her marriage a year-long exhausting fight.

'Please listen to me…' Angie lowered her stubborn guard because she knew that she had to, her voice trembling as she did so. 'I can—'

'No.' He turned around again, and the moment she

looked into his face she felt a wave of sick apprehension riddle her stomach. 'Not this time, Angie. This time you are going to listen to *me.*'

He strode back to the desk and opened the drawer again. With a graceful flick of his long fingers he produced a folder which he set down on the desk. *'Angie'*, it said, in his own sharp scrawl on the label. That was all—just *'Angie'*—yet seeing her name written there made Angie feel slightly sick.

Opening the dossier and flicking through the pages until he found what he was looking for, Roque then spun the whole thing round and sent it sliding across the desk, so it came to a neat stop in front of her.

Mouth so dry now it felt as if she'd been eating sand, her eyelashes fluttered, and she looked down and began to read. Her heart started to thump as she tallied up the column of figures on the right hand side of a long list of transactions going back months and months. It was only when she saw confirmation of the horrifying total at the bottom of the third page that she finally—finally—blanched.

Roque was silent. He just stood there and let her discover how deeply her brother had thrown her into debt to him. She could not even look at him. Horror and shame sent her trembling fingers flicking back and forth through the pages in the vague hope that she'd mis-tallied the figures—then it suddenly dawned on her.

'Angie'...

She looked up. 'You thought it was me, didn't you?' she breathed unsteadily.

'At first.' Roque nodded. 'I thought you were trying

to force a response out of me, so I decided to play along and see how far...'

His voice tailed off to an expressive grimace, leaving Angie to fill in the bit he'd left out. Forever the strategist, she thought bleakly.

'So you could have nipped Alex's stupidity in the bud a whole lot sooner?' Angie concluded thickly. 'Thanks for nothing, Roque.'

'It was not mere stupidity, Angie. It was theft!' Roque thrust out the hard distinction. 'And when did you ever allow me any say over what your brother did?' he added harshly. 'I was the interloper in my own marriage. If I uttered a complaint you went off the deep end. If I offered advice you threw it back in my face. Well, this time it will be different.' Reaching over, he drew the dossier back to his side of the desk. 'This time I will have control of what this represents, Angie, and you are going to have to swallow your frankly annoying stubbornness and deal with that.'

The way he stabbed a long finger at the damning bank statements made Angie blink and her eyes started to sting. 'But—but you know I will get you the money,' she choked in confusion. 'Why are you making such a meal out of this?'

'Because,' Roque stated, 'it is not your debt.'

'But it is!' she insisted. '*My* credit card! *My* name on the bills! I know you can't have a leg to stand on. I just need time to check that out with a lawyer or something, but—'

'Or we could bring in the police and let them decide.'

'Or I could change my divorce plea.' Angie went in for the kill, because she had nothing else left to fight him with. 'And go for half of everything you own, citing your adultery with Nadia!'

Roque heaved in a breath.

'Go for it,' he invited, his fabulous bone structure hard as nails now, 'and I will have your brother arrested. Make no mistake about it. This is called a stalemate, Angie, in case you have not yet worked it out.'

What it was, Angie thought, was Roque throwing down the gauntlet between them. He might as well have slapped her with it, hard in the face!

Dropping the pen, she stepped back from the desk with a jerk. 'So why have you brought me here if you are not prepared to negotiate with me?' she demanded in a hurt, bewildered voice.

Her long, slender frame so taut that it trembled, her hands clenched into white-knuckled fists at her sides, she might sound bewildered and hurt, but she still had enough spirit left in her to fling back her head, Roque noted dryly as, within the circle of light from the overhead desk light, he watched her shimmer like a firecracker about to go off.

Without needing to think about his answer, he went with his instincts and strode around that light pool until he was standing directly in front of her—towering over her as intimidating as hell.

'I brought you here for this,' he murmured ever so succinctly, lifting up one of his long-fingered hands to rest it warm against her throat.

'Don't you dare!' she seethed, knowing what was coming.

Oh, he dared. Angie tried to push him away, but Roque had that covered. He planted his other hand on the base of her spine and drew her inexorably against him.

Anticipation as to what was about to happen sent fiery sparks showering down over Angie's flesh. Everything about him was big and hard and familiar, like making contact with something precious she'd lost.

'I hate you,' she whispered in a last ditch attempt to save herself.

He just hit her with one of his mocking smiles because he knew—oh, how well he knew—what she was really fighting.

Then he wasn't smiling. He was parting his lips and bringing them down into burning contact with hers. She stiffened her whole body and trembled in her determination to feel nothing. She tried—tried not to give any kind of response. But then he made that slow, sensuous glide with his tongue across her lips, and on the back of an unforgivable shiver of pleasure she surrendered. She surrendered like a fool with no brain and let her lips fall apart in an invitation he accepted with the hot, stabbing thrust of his tongue.

She drowned in that kiss for a full thirty seconds. She let him drive her wild as the natural firecracker living inside her went off with passionate force. It spun her back into a world she had tried so hard not to remember—the feel of him, the glorious taste, the urgent trampling heat of desire he could create inside her so quickly, which flung her from icy with hatred to hot with desire without a gap in between. Her fingers clawed up his shirt-front, making him shudder as her nails raked flesh covered only by the thinness of his shirt, then wince when they dug like talons into the back of his neck.

Roque jerked his head up. *'Gatinho,'* he muttered.

The little cat inside Angie purred with angry triumph,

then went for the kill with a lethal precision he really should have been ready for. She sank her teeth into his full and pulsing sexy lower lip. With a grinding growl of reaction he bent her into such an acute arch that she cried out. The next thing she knew he was kissing her so deeply she lost the ability to do anything else but cling. Her heart went crazy, another anxious, helpless moan sounded deep in her throat, and her breasts were crushed against his chest now, their dusky pink tips stirring and tightening to sensitive pinpricks. If it hadn't been for her coat he would have felt them. As it was he just kissed her until she gave back with a melting urgency she was thoroughly ashamed of even while she couldn't stop herself from doing it.

Roque drew back his head and looked down into the dazed shimmer of her eyes, then at her full, hot, pulsing mouth. With a sensual arrogance he lowered his head again to slide his tongue across its quivering width. Angie released a helpless little whimper. He repeated the stroke and finished it with a deeply erotic tangling with her tongue before he lifted up his head again.

Smouldering dark eyes burned a cruelly implacable look down at her, 'This,' he said, ever so softly, 'is your only negotiating chip, *minha doce*. Take it or leave it.'

Then, with a coolness that stunned Angie into a deep freeze, he put her away from him, stepped around her, and strode for the door.

Reeling around to watch him go, every inch of his long, powerful body in such perfect harmony, Angie cringed inside with the flaming heat of her own humiliation for being so weak as to let him do this to her.

'To listen to you anyone would think you were lily-white and perfect,' she flung after him shakily. 'But you were unfaithful to me, Roque. Does that count for anything with you?'

Roque stilled on the threshold, the breadth of his shoulders revealing only the slightest hint of a tense twitch. 'It counted for something twelve months ago, when you deserved an explanation and redress from me but refused both. Now it is too late. I will give you neither. So take my advice and get over it, Angie. This is a different time, with different issues. Get a grip and move on.'

Get a grip and move on…?

Angie released a strangled little laugh that made those shoulders hunch a second time as he continued out of the room.

'Get a grip and move on' from the sight of the man you loved heart and soul wrapped in the arms of another woman? Not in this lifetime—or even in the next life, come to that. He'd broken her heart. He'd wrecked her ability to believe in herself.

The first time she'd met Roque had been at a London fashion shoot. Tall, dark, just too gorgeous to be real. She'd automatically assumed he was one of the brooding male models turning up for the shoot. It was a few minutes later when Nadia Sanchez, an exotic dark Brazilian model, went to wind herself around him and she realised that he must be the latest lover Nadia had been going on about like a fluttery love-sick bird.

'Don't you know who he is?' another model had whispered. 'That's Roque de Calvhos, the most gorgeous, sexiest, richest playboy bachelor out there!'

And he'd been staring directly at Angie as if Nadia wasn't standing there, showering his handsome face with kisses. Roque had lost his chance to make an impact on her right there and then. She had no time for smooth, self-obsessed love-rats who thought nothing of eyeing up other women while his current lover poured adoration over him with an enthusiasm he obviously believed he deserved. And anyway, she'd already had too many other things to think about without adding the unexpected problem of the swift, unwanted hot flare of attraction she'd suffered as her eyes had made contact with his.

So she'd turned her back on him and hadn't let herself glance that way again until she was sure he had left, with Nadia still clinging to him, blissfully unaware that she'd just been insulted by the very man she was no doubt about to go to bed with.

Within hours she'd made herself forget all about him. So when he'd called her at her hotel that same evening and introduced himself it had taken her several seconds to connect with the name.

'I would like to take you to dinner,' he expressed, in a dark accented voice that oozed with the sensual self-confidence that she was about to jump on his neck with gratitude and delight.

She told him bluntly where to stick his invitation and cut the connection. When the flowers arrived ten minutes later she returned them with a note.

Let's get a couple of things straight, Mr Calvhos. I don't go out with love-rats and I don't cheat on my colleagues. Take my name and number out of your little black book and don't contact me again.

'*De* Calvhos,' he corrected lazily by telephone the next day. 'And little black books became obsolete with the arrival of the BlackBerry.'

'And I'm running late for my flight to New York,' she responded, before cutting him off once more.

She'd done the full fashion circuit and was right here in London before they met up again. She and Nadia had not crossed paths since the last London shoot, so when the other model arrived for London Fashion Week Angie was already on her guard, expecting Roque to appear at any moment. She spotted him front of house, sitting next to Carla, and she seethed all the way down the runway and back up it again—because she could feel his dark eyes lazily undressing her from the flimsy scrap of multi-coloured silk she was wearing as if he had the right. But what really disturbed her was the thought that she'd probably been undressed like that a thousand times before without ever noticing.

Making the clothes look fabulously sexy and alluring was her job. Full-stop. She didn't want to feel Roque's eyes doing that to her. She didn't want to know she could be susceptible to any man's glance.

After the show he arrived backstage with Carla on his arm. Smooth and sleek, and infuriatingly sure of himself, he used the only person Angie could call a friend to assure a formal introduction between the two of them. When he wanted them to, Roque's charmingly polite manners could melt an iceberg. Shame it was spoiled by Nadia, who came to wind herself around his other arm like a slinky dark sex kitten with a hot siren's smile.

Angie was actually happy to have her mobile phone burst into life, with her brother's headmaster on the other end of it informing her Alex had been taken to hospital after a brawl with another pupil had knocked him out. She made hurried excuses and rushed out of the reception, her attention fixed on finding a taxi that would take her to Hampshire.

Roque appeared at her side as she was begging a black cab driver to make the journey. 'Come on.' He took hold of her arm. 'My car is parked over here. I will take you.'

The beginning of the end of her resistance to him, Angie thought now with a bitter wry smile. The breathtaking patience with which he'd dealt with her prickly hostility even as she'd let him drive her all the way to the hospital local to Alex's school. The way he'd waited patiently while she'd checked that her brother was not at death's door and dealt with his censorious headmaster because her brother had apparently started the brawl.

Limp as a rag by the time they'd started the journey back to London again, and in snappish mood, she'd reminded him that he'd left Nadia standing back in London.

'Nadia and I have not been an item since I first saw you,' he'd stated coolly. Then, with a deliberate change of subject, 'Tell me about your parents. Why are they not here to deal with your brother?'

And that had been it. For some reason Angie still could not figure that quietly serious question had ended her objections to him. For the first time since she'd taken responsibility for Alex she'd found herself pouring it all out on that car journey back to London. By the time he'd seen her safely inside her Chelsea apartment she had already been halfway infatuated by his quiet manner and his seriously disturbing charm.

Angie sighed, narrow shoulders hunching inside her coat as she slumped down onto the edge of Roque's desk and stared down her long legs at her flat-shoed feet. Within a week he had been her lover. Within three months he'd asked her to marry him. Within a year all her rose-tinted dreams had lain broken—more than broken—*shattered* by a sequence of nightmarish events she still found impossible to think about, though the hurt they'd inflicted refused to hide away with the thoughts.

'Take off the coat.'

Lifting up her head, Angie was not quick enough to cover up those feelings her memories brought back. She hurt. She *hurt*. And he was lounging there, at ease in the doorway, arms folded across his shirt-front, eyes slightly narrowed, watching her steadily.

In charge.

She dragged her eyes away from him. 'When I look at you I see Nadia,' she told him bleakly.

'When I look at you I see a blind, stubborn woman,' he drawled back. 'Stop fighting me, Angie,' he then said flatly. 'Your year-long sulking time is up. Accept it.'

Sulking? He dared to think she was merely *sulking*?

'I just don't want to be in your life any more!' Hating that she was revealing even this one small glimpse of vulnerability to him, Angie shot away from the desk.

'But you will be in my life again,' Roque returned, smooth as glass, 'because, *meu querida*, baby brother expects you to do whatever it is I want you to do.'

He was challenging her to deny it. To call his bluff. In one dark corner of her agonised feelings Angie even suspected that he wanted her to walk away.

Power games, she recognised. Not with her this time, but with Alex. He wanted her to leave her brother to face up to his crimes for himself.

'I don't even understand why you want me back.' She was genuinely mystified by that. 'It's not as if you enjoyed living with me the first time around.'

His mouth gave a twitch. 'You had your good moments.'

Angie uttered a low husky laugh. 'You can get good sex anywhere, Roque, and without having to put up with the hassle of a pain-in-the-neck wife breathing all over your guilty conscience.'

'I don't have a guilty conscience.'

'Well, you should have!' she flared. 'You took Nadia to bed. You had great sex with her. The newspapers were *full* of how good it was. So don't you *dare* stand there and admit to me that you don't feel guilty about it when it was me they ridiculed because I could not keep my husband happy!'

'Well, did you—keep me happy?'

Seeing the arched eyebrows which accompanied his calm counter-charge, Angie saw no hint—not even a glimpse of a hint—of regret in his hard, handsome face.

She pulled in a breath, feeling an unwanted pressure building up in her chest. No, she had not kept Roque happy. But when had he bothered to make an effort to make *her* happy?

He'd complained about her job commitments. He'd complained about Alex. Every decision she'd had to make about her brother he had opposed. When she'd tried to make him understand her point of view he'd grown impatient with her and walked off. Sometimes she'd felt so lonely and confused she'd hidden in the bathroom and wept.

'I'm hungry,' he said. 'Are you going or staying?'

He was thinking about food while she was killing herself with their miserable past? Angie folded her arms and did not answer. A burning resentment sizzled in her blood. The silence stretched—she stretched it—until Roque decided to make it snap.

'Are you going or staying?' he repeated.

'Staying!' Angie burst out with a whip-cracking fury that should have brought the walls tumbling down around them both.

Roque winced as he pushed away from the door-frame and strode further into the room. The air between them crackled and fizzed with the echoing effects of her burst of fury. Angie was actually breathing fast in the aftermath, but without saying another word Roque just reached for her arms, calmly unfolded them, then set about untying the belt on her coat.

'You would not become this agitated if you were not such a control freak,' he opined, with all the diplomacy of a superior being talking down to a mulish child.

Raising her eyes to send him a swift acid glance she hoped would sear off a layer of his golden skin, she noticed the swelling in the centre of his lower lip and was suddenly overtaken by remorse. By the look of it she had a horrible feeling she had actually drawn blood.

'I'm—sorry,' she husked. 'About the...' She lifted a finger as if to touch his lip, then curled the projecting finger into her fist, dropped her hand again and made do with a shrug.

As if he wanted to make her suffer, he ran the tip of his tongue over the swelling with such lazy sensuality Angie felt as if she was suddenly drowning in static.

'I *really* hate you,' she choked, as if the declaration was going to make the feeling go away.

It didn't.

Sliding a hand inside her coat, he laid the flat of his palm against the base of her long, supple spine, then used his long fingers to exert pressure to ease her up from the desk. She arrived a short whisper away from the hard-packed warmth of his body and her inner sizzle just got worse. Like a silly, breathless, tense little whippet she dropped her eyes from his mouth to stare at the triangle of tanned skin left exposed by the open collar of his shirt and let him ease her coat from her shoulders, then toss it across the desk. Tears were pressing at her. Her heart felt like a huge aching lump in her chest.

'I won't have sex with you.' As if she was mesmerised by that golden-brown triangle of skin, her declaration had arrived on the back of her wanting to lean and press her lips against it then stretch up to do the same to his beautiful bruised lip.

He caught hold of her hand and said absolutely nothing. What Roque could do with silence should be bottled and sold, Angie decided, as she wimped out of fighting to get her hand back and let him lead her across the room.

He knew why she'd just blurted out her last comment. He knew she'd never been able to stand close to him without wanting to devour him alive. Roque was her one confessed weakness. Not his mind, not his wealth, not his gorgeous looks, nor even the warm and exciting charm he could turn on occasionally.

No, she lusted after his body, full-stop.

But she didn't love him any more, she told herself.

She didn't.

She let him trail her behind him across the wide open space that made up the seating area of soft black leather sofas set around a black marble wall-fire, currently licking with flames behind a plate of glass. It was dark outside now. London was twinkling. He brought her into the spacious kitchen bay, where Angie picked up on the delicious aroma of something spicy for the first time.

She'd eaten nothing since a snatched lunch consisting of an apple and a yogurt, so her nostrils flared hungrily and her stomach gave a timely growl.

Propping her up against one of the shiny black kitchen units, Roque turned away to cross over to a giant-sized cooking range. Angie frowned, curious, because of all the things Roque was infuriatingly good at, cooking wasn't one of them. He could manage to put together a grilled bacon sandwich if he absolutely had to, or throw some salad between two slices of bread, but cooking— real cooking, the likes of which was giving off the delicious aromas she was picking up—came under the heading of 'Professional Chefs' or an assortment of favoured good restaurants as far as Roque was concerned.

Had he changed his mind and brought staff in here to take care of him? Mrs Grant came in daily, to keep the apartment in order, but she had never been expected to cook. Still frowning, Angie watched the under-cupboard lighting reflect down onto his long brown fingers as he lifted the lid off a pan of what looked like simmering pasta.

'You made that?' She could not stop herself from asking the question.

'From a packet,' he admitted, 'with precise instructions printed on it. The rest came ready-cooked in cartons from Gino's.' He named a local Italian bistro they'd used to eat at often. 'Gino refused to provide his fresh pasta for me to ruin.'

Flipping open the door to the microwave, he removed a sealed carton and almost burnt his fingers in the process. With a cursing *ouch*, he dropped the hot carton down on the granite counter. Fighting with herself not to do it, in the end Angie sighed and walked forward to pick up a teatowel, then silently shoved him out of the way.

A few minutes later Gino's best savoury sauce had been blended with steaming pasta, and a mound of succulently spicy meatballs was heaped on the top. Refusing to glance at Roque, who now leant casually against the counter-top content to watch her finish what he had started, Angie picked up the serving dish and turned to transport it to the small dining table set in front of one of the floor-to-ceiling windows next to the kitchen. There was another table in the more formal dining area—a grand-looking antique imported from his native Portugal, like the desk, but it had rarely been used by them unless they'd had guests for dinner, which hadn't been often because their time schedules always...

Angie stopped that train of thinking before it eroded this temporary calm they seemed to have reached without her knowing how they had done it.

The small table was already set for two, which almost—almost—brought a smile to her lips, because setting a table was one of the few domestic chores Roque could undertake. Or *would* undertake, she amended as she set the dish down in the middle of the table.

'Exquisite,' he murmured.

'Of course it is. Gino made it,' Angie said as she straightened up.

'*Meu Deus*, I was not referring to the food,' he husked, bringing her gaze swinging round and up to his face.

CHAPTER FOUR

ANGIE felt suddenly as if she was suffocating. A sizzle of self-awareness imprisoned her breath. He was looking at what she was wearing, his too-dark eyes coming alive with a glow which highlighted their true rich brown colour as he swept them down over her black mini-skirt splashed with emerald-green dots teamed with a flimsy black chiffon top.

A low drumbeat of tension began to throb between them as Roque followed the way the skirt clung to her tiny waist and fell in soft gathers three-quarters of the way up her lengthy thighs. Without the matt black tights the skirt would be indecent. With the tights what that tiny skirt did for the length of her legs was nothing short of sensational. What the flimsy top did for the high, firm rounded breasts he could see moving behind the gauzy fabric was, however, a different thing entirely, and his reaction was striking directly at the raw, macho and possessive heart of him.

He knew she worked on the front desk at CGM Management. He knew by the timing that she must have rushed like mad to get over here as quickly as she had. But the thought of his wife tripping around CGM's vast white marble reception area all day wearing this outfit ignited his primitive side. Her hair was a shiny mass of silky red spirals clinging to her narrow shoulders; her legs went on for ever inside those matt black tights. If she had walked in here stark naked she could not have turned him on as hard and as fast as this outfit was doing right now. He wanted to lift her up so she could wrap those long legs around him. His wanted to sink his head down and suck on those twin peaks he could see pressing invitingly against the lace outline of the top.

She was his. She belonged to him. His long, tall, sexy bride who'd almost got away from him. He wanted to haul her upstairs and stamp his claim on her so thoroughly she would never want to get away from him again.

'Stop it,' she choked.

'Stop what?' he growled in hungry response.

That, Angie wanted to say as that hungry growl made itself felt in the stinging tips of her breasts and the clamouring juncture of her thighs.

'Do you want to eat this food or not?' She turned away again, and caught the sound of his exhaled breath.

'At least the big green bag suddenly makes sense,' he murmured, a trifle whimsically.

Refusing to take that whimsy on, she said, 'It came with the outfit,' pulling out a chair for herself and sitting down on it quickly when Roque made a move to do the polite thing and hold the chair for her. 'And it's an old one,' she added—because it was the truth. 'I bought it last year, after I…'

The rest of what she had been about to say just froze into a lump in her throat. Angie dipped her head down, appalled with herself for almost blurting out what she had.

A silence developed—a thick one, with aching undertones that contracted the walls of her chest. The lowest point of her life, she thought bleakly. Even lower than the moment she'd discovered that Roque had cheated on her.

'Where did you go when you hid away from me?' The quiet question arrived from across the table, and she looked up to find Roque had sat down at the table without her even realising it.

'Nowhere.' Dropping her eyes from his again, she attempted an indifferent shrug while making a play of smoothing the folds of her skirt.

'I looked for you,' he said almost roughly. 'I looked for you everywhere, but you just seemed to disappear off the face of the earth.'

'When—when you have a relatively well-known face you have to disappear off the face of the earth if you don't want to be found,' Angie pointed out, with what she hoped was a cool dryness aimed to cover up what she was really feeling.

Roque grimaced as he served food onto their plates. 'A convent, perhaps?' he suggested. Then, 'No,' he mused thoughtfully. 'I had all the convents checked out. Same with the hotels…*all* holistic retreats. I began scraping the barrel when I started checking the hospitals—but I suppose that you find it highly satisfying to know you worried me like— What?' he demanded sharply when Angie turned white.

Staring at the plate of steaming food sitting in front of her, Angie felt her stomach contract. Her legs were tingling with an urgent need to get up and run away from what he'd said. She did not want to remember her three long months of self-imposed isolation—or the other month she'd spent confined to a hospital bed.

Across the table Roque was frowning, tracking back over what he had said that could have put that terrible expression on her face.

'Angie—'

'I don't want to talk about it.' Reaching out blindly, she picked up her wine glass—only to find it was empty when she raised it to her lips.

Smothering an urge to growl in frustration, Roque picked up the wine bottle and stretched across the table to take her glass from her, so he could fill it up.

By then Angie had dared to look at him. She saw the controlled volcano he was grimly keeping banked down because she refused to open up to him, and wished, for a split second, that he wasn't her enemy.

'Thanks,' she mumbled when he offered back the wine glass. A delicate sip or two later and the tense clutch of nausea had eased its grip on her stomach.

She picked up her knife and fork and made herself eat, taking tiny mouthfuls which tasted divine but were still difficult to swallow. Roque did the same. When, seemingly, they'd both had enough of pretending they were enjoying the meal, he sat back with a sigh, and Angie leapt on the moment by standing up and reaching across the table to pick up his plate.

Once again he took her by complete surprise, grabbing hold of her wrist.

'What now?' she demanded, watching another frown descend over his face.

'Your rings,' he said. 'You are not wearing your rings.'

'Of course I'm not.' She snatched her wrist back. 'I

took them off when you stopped being a faithful husband to me and…'

Her snappy voice trailed away to a strangled nothing when it suddenly hit her what they were actually talking about, and she just froze to a breathless effigy where she stood.

Her rings.

'Oh, my God.' Her mind went into total freefall.

Her rings!

If her brother could calmly lift a credit card from her bedside drawer and swan off to use it, then what about the other things she'd stuffed in the drawer with it?

Moving on legs which felt vaguely fluffy now, she stepped away from the table and ran across the apartment into Roque's study. A few seconds later she was rushing back out again, with her bag swinging from her fingers while she struggled to drag on her coat.

'Where do you think you're going?' Roque demanded.

Angie hovered halfway between the lobby and the table, where he now stood looking like an angry black cloud about to pour down on her head.

'I…need to go back to my flat.' Knowing she must look as white as a sheet, because she felt as if she did, she moistened her dry trembling mouth. 'I think I l-left something on—the cooker. I…'

Lying didn't come easy to her, and by his face Roque knew she was lying through her chattering white teeth. But she didn't dare say out loud what she was thinking. She didn't dare bring her brother's name back into this.

'I'll come back,' she promised, and started moving

again, quickly, like a prisoner trying for escape. 'When—when I've—'

'I'm coming with you.'

'No!' Taut as a stretch of wire, the refusal almost scraped the lining off her throat. 'I can grab a cab—' She hit the lift's call button. 'You don't have to—'

Roque's hand on the base of her spine propelled into the lift carriage, 'Stop taking me for a fool, Angie,' he bit out as he sent them sinking down. 'Whatever it is that just spooked you, I want to know about it.'

'Nothing has spooked me! I just remembered I might have left a pan on the cooker!'

'Liar,' he rasped, and that was it as far as he was concerned.

The lift doors slid open onto the basement car park. He guided her to his midnight-blue Porsche and saw her inside it with such grim precision Angie had to scramble inelegantly to fold in her long legs.

She dared a swift glance up at his hard profile. 'I might not have done.' She decided she'd better cover herself, ready for the moment when her lie was exposed. 'I'm just not sure. But I have to go and—'

'Shut up.' Roque shut the door.

By the time he joined her his temper was on such a fine trigger Angie decided to take his advice.

They drove across London in absolute silence, Angie growing more tense and anxious the closer they came to her flat. She was out of the car before Roque had even stopped it, scrambling in her bag for her keys while she hurried to get the door open before he arrived. In her tiny hallway it took only two strides for her to reach her bedroom. Trembling lips pressed together, she walked over to her bedside cabinet and slid open the drawer, then just stood looking down at its contents through eyes that stung.

All kinds of small things were scattered in the drawer. She had not seen or thought about them in months. But it was a small box her fingers reached for, and with a heavy thump playing havoc with her heartbeat she pulled in a taut breath, then flipped open the lid.

Two rings winked back at her. One an intricately woven rich yellow gold wedding ring Roque had had to have altered to make it fit the narrowness of her finger. It was a family heirloom, passed down the line through the de Calvhos brides for too many centuries for her to dare to count. The same with the betrothal ring, with its fabulously rare pink diamond gleaming like a lustrous living thing from a bed of exquisite white diamonds.

She'd meant to return the rings to Roque when she'd returned to London, but she'd pushed them into this drawer along with the credit card and promptly forgotten about them.

Wanted to forget about them.

Needed to forget about them.

Though now, as she stared at these priceless and irreplaceable pieces from the de Calvhos jewellery stock, guilt made a fierce grab at her conscience for the way she had just tossed them into this drawer as if they were worth nothing.

Her brother had missed the jackpot when he'd left the rings behind, she thought helplessly, for the pink diamond alone would have paid off his debts, with an obscene amount left over for him to squander further.

A spike of hot bloody anger held Roque still in the doorway. It wasn't because of the rings. The rings were still there—he could see them sparkling in the box from here. It was having to witness Angie's fear that her brother had taken them that was infuriating him.

Without saying a word, he walked forward, then bent to ease the ring box out of her grasp. She flinched when he snapped the box shut and closed it inside his clenched fist.

'Okay.' He sounded harsh, but couldn't help it. 'Now we are here, you can pack a bag before we leave again.'

'He—he didn't do it, Roque,' Angie whispered.

'What the hell difference does that make?' he exploded, without knowing he was going to do that either. 'You believed he was capable of stealing your rings from you, Angie! You are sitting there like that, fighting back the tears, because you are so relieved that he did not! Now, pack a damn bag!'

'Don't shout at me!' Angie sprang to her feet and glared at him.

'Do you need me to spell it out to you before you recognise what's going on here?' he rasped. 'The rings do not matter. The credit card he took matters! If we let him get away with what he has done, what do you think he's going to take next? Or, worse, who is he going to steal from to finance his gambling habit?'

'It's not gambling!' Angie heard herself repeat Alex's own defence from a hazy place filled with horror and self-disgust. 'Y-you speculate on the markets all the time, Roque, and I've never heard you call it gambling.'

'I do not steal from other people to do it. I do not drag my family down to a level where they are forced to defend me like you are doing now—just to save his face!'

Guilty as charged, Angie quivered out a pained, shaken breath. 'He's all I've got and I love him.'

It came out so bleak and so broken that Roque swung away in a lithe, angry movement to glare at the nearest wall with a burning desire to throw his clenched fist at it!

And he knew why he felt like that. Hell, did he know.

'Where is his love for you, Angie?' He swung back to her, grinding his teeth together when he watched her flinch. 'He walks all over you—because you let him. How long do you think the rings would have remained in that drawer if what he's been doing with the credit card had not been exposed? Do you think he did not notice the ring box?' he pushed on relentlessly, even as she dropped weakly back onto the bed.

'He resisted the rings because the credit card was easier. He has more nous than you, *meu querida*, because I think he worked it out that selling the famous de Calvhos diamond would bring him more trouble than it was worth. And what the *hell* were you doing, tossing such a valuable object into a drawer as if it was a cheap piece of junk?'

'I know.' On an agonised groan she lifted up a hand to cover her face. 'I'm very sorry.'

Roque released a growl like an angry and frustrated snarling animal. The atmosphere in the room hit incendiary levels because he did not want her apology—he wanted—

Ramming the ring box into his pocket, he reached down and lifted her back to her feet. 'Okay,' he said, 'this is what is going to happen.' He gave her a gentle shake in case she wasn't listening to him. 'You are going to pack a bag and come back home with me.'

The *home* bit sent her lips parting and her chest rising on an intake of air, ready to object.

'Then,' he continued uncompromisingly, 'there is going to be a new order of things in our marriage, where I take full control of your brother and you willingly hand that control over to me.'

'If you hurt Alex in any way I will never forgive you!' Angie instantly choked out.

'I don't want to hurt him. I want to teach him how to be a man before it's too damn late!'

When she blinked, as if he'd shocked the hell out of her, Roque made himself tug in a controlling breath.

'I will tell you something, Angie,' he continued, less harshly. 'I think Alex craves to be taught that lesson. I saw the need burning in his eyes when we faced up to each other today. He hates me, but he would love to be me—why do you think he chose to gamble on the stockmarkets in this current financial climate, when only the hardy dare touch it? I am his role model. The only successful male role model he's had any real contact with. He would have loved to have thrown the credit card and a stack of profited money at me and then told me to go to hell today.'

'Instead you sent him to m-me, with his tail between his legs.'

'Exactly where his tail deserved to be,' Roque delivered without a hint of regret. 'It was his first lesson in facing up to his actions.'

To her own surprise, Angie let out a strangled snatch of a laugh. 'You would not be saying that if you'd heard what he had to say about you.'

'I'm a big boy. I can take his insults.'

'At a price.' Angie slipped out of his grasp and moved away from him.

As if someone had cued the precise moment it was to happen, her phone starting ringing. Turning back to the bed, where she'd dropped her bag when she'd come in here, Angie hunted through it and came out with her mobile phone.

'It's Alex.' She knew that it would be. 'I promised to—'

'Don't answer it.'

About to connect with the call, Angie lifted her head up in shock. 'But he—'

'Let him stew.'

There was a stony cool in the way Roque said that which sent a chill chasing down Angie's back. Her fingertip hovered over the appropriate button on the phone, but her gaze clung to Roque's grim, hard and inflexible expression while she battled with a desire to defy his instruction and the helpless knowledge that he was right.

As if Roque had planned this whole wretched scene, a police car's siren whined past her bedroom window as it sped down the street. In her hand her phone sang out its insistent melody, and her mouth began to tremble, her eyes began to sting.

On a hiss of impatience, as if he wasn't happy at all about what he was going to do next, Roque reached out and took the phone from her. 'I will talk to him.'

Was that supposed to make her feel better? 'Please, Roque.' Angie burst into speech. 'Don't—'

'Pack that bag.' He turned with her phone and strode out of her bedroom.

Left standing there, Angie listened as the ringing stopped, then Roque's deep, smooth-accented voice murmured with excruciating casualness, *'Boa tarde*, Alex. Your sister is busy right now. Can I be of help?' before the bedroom door swung shut.

She packed an overnight bag with the mindless inefficiency of someone who did not care what she packed. She did not pack more than she needed for an overnight stay—refused to. Refused to think beyond this one horrible night.

By the time she'd hauled the holdall strap over her shoulder and scooped up her green bag, Roque was striding back into the bedroom again with the long, loose-limbed grace of a man in control of everything—even his body. Angie sizzled with the desire to take a swing at him with the heaviest bag and knock the over-confident devil off his self-assured plinth.

'Ready to leave?'

Pressing her lips together, she said nothing, knowing if she opened her mouth at all she would be begging him to tell her what he'd said to her brother—and she refused to give him the satisfaction of seeing how completely she felt she was dancing to his tune.

He reached out to lift her holdall off her shoulder, then really surprised her by offering her back her mobile phone.

'Don't you want to put it in your desk drawer alongside my chequebook?' she asked him tartly.

'Don't put ideas in my head.'

Angie snatched the phone from him and plunged it to the bottom of the green bag. Roque did not bother to tell her he had switched it off before handing it back. Switched-off phones did not hand out temptation to use them, and he wasn't comfortably sure he had eased her brother's panic.

He offered up information. 'I have set up a meeting with Alex for tomorrow.'

Bright head tilted down, Angie cinched the belt even tighter to her tiny waist, as if the coat was a piece of armour she could use to protect herself from him.

No chance, Roque thought. 'What happens at the meeting depends entirely on you,' he added, soft and goading as a sharp fingernail being drawn down the skin of her back.

Shoving past him, she walked into the hallway, leaving him to grimace as he followed her outside. They drove back to his apartment in sizzling silence and entered it in silence. By then the time had gone way beyond midnight, and Angie felt as if she was about to drop where she stood. Turning around and almost bumping into Roque, because he was so close behind her, she kept her eyes firmly lowered from his hard, handsome face while she took her holdall from him.

'Goodnight,' she said, then walked off towards the stairs.

Once again Roque said nothing, and she dragged that nothing with her all the way up the staircase onto the mezzanine above. She'd already said her piece about their sleeping arrangements, she reminded herself stubbornly. It did not need repeating.

She did not look down to where she knew he stood, watching her every single step of the way. She refused to give the ever-present tears she could feel pushing at the back of her throat room to vent. She chose a bedroom as far away from their old shared bedroom as she could possibly put herself. Dropping her bags down on the chaise at the end of the bed, she unzipped the holdall, fished out a set of hastily packed pink silk pyjamas and her soap bag, then headed for the bathroom.

Ten minutes later she was crawling beneath a fluffy white duvet with her mind turned into a stubborn blank.

Ten minutes after that Roque trod silently into the same bedroom and came to stand looking down at her, a wry, slightly regretful expression on his face.

She was just a curled-up mound beneath the duvet, topped by a glossy mass of copper curls spread out behind her on the pillow, and she was well and truly out for the count. Watching the gentle rise and fall of her breathing, he wondered what kind of rat would want to disturb her from such a deep slumber.

This rat, he answered his own question. There was no way he was going to ease up on Angie in this new order of things he had mapped out.

Drawing his hands out of the pockets of his bathrobe, he bent down and gently scooped her and the duvet up into his arms. She stirred with a complaining sigh which sent him still for a second, his arms tensing in readiness for a fight. But she just settled more comfortably into his shoulder, and he got his first good look at her sleeping face. A rush of feeling sank down through his torso as he gazed at her softly parted lips. The urge to dip his head and claim that mouth almost got the better of him—until he grimly curbed the urge and turned instead to head out of the room.

Angie felt as if she was floating. She felt warm and comfy and safe. She turned her head so she could nuzzle the pillow, and dreamed she was nuzzling Roque's warm throat.

That dream again, she thought with a sigh, and then dreamed up the soft hiss that Roque always used to let her know he was becoming aroused. One day, she vowed, she would find someone else to dream about who would wipe Roque de Calvhos clean out of her head.

Then she shivered as her floating body touched down onto something cool and the duvet was summarily stripped away, bringing her awake with a start. Her eyes flew open, hot and gritty. She threw a sleepily confused glance down the length of the bed, where the duvet now lay neatly folded beneath her feet. Bewildered as to how it had got there, Angie stretched down to grab it. She had just managed to haul it up to her chin when a sound sent her head twisting on the pillow to discover that Roque was standing right there beside the bed, calmly stripping off a navy blue robe.

Heart banging against her ribs, 'What do you think you are doing in here?' she tossed at him.

CHAPTER FIVE

'COMING to bed,' Roque murmured impassively.

Angie clutched the duvet all the tighter. 'Not with me, you're not!'

His response was to cast the robe aside with the casual grace of silent intent. He was wearing nothing beneath it, not a single solitary stitch, and was so absolutely carelessly at home with his naked beauty he just stood there and let her look her fill.

Angie's mouth dried up. The helpless need to reacquaint herself with every familiar contour sent her eyes drinking in every glossy square inch. The satin bronze power in his wide shoulders. The sleek bulging biceps in his upper arms. She made a sweeping scan of the steel-plate formation of his hair-peppered torso down to the corded bowl of his narrow hips to where he didn't even care that he was displaying the rampant fullness of his arousal. A fire lit down deep in her belly, and she wriggled her bottom and clutched more tightly on the duvet.

'Y-you agreed,' she whispered.

'I agreed to nothing,' he denied, flipping up the duvet with the clear intention of climbing beneath it.

Angie whipped across to the other side of the bed

like a sidewinder. It was as she did so that she noticed the other duvet, lying in a fluffy mound of white on the floor, and belatedly took in her surroundings.

'You moved me!' she gasped.

'You sleep where I sleep.' Stretching out beside her, he yawned widely, then spread out an arm to douse the light. 'Now, be quiet and go to sleep. I'm shattered.'

He was shattered? Angie had not been awake past ten o'clock for months, and her head was spinning with exhaustion. Throwing herself around to glare at him while he made himself comfortable, she considered climbing back out of the bed again, then changed her mind. She was so tired her legs felt as if they'd been pinned to the mattress by lead weights. She could barely keep her gritty eyes open, and she had a dull, aching thump happening in her head. And if she did get up she knew he would only bring her back again.

On a sound of disgust, she yanked a pillow out from beneath her head and rammed it down the middle of the bed. 'If your skin so much as touches my skin, even accidentally while you sleep, I will give you another thick lip,' she threatened, thumping her remaining pillow before dropping her head down on it.

A stunning silence followed that declaration. Angie shut her eyes tight and built fabulous images behind her closed eyelids of her suddenly gaining super-human strength and knocking out the over-muscled, over-endowed brute. It was such a very satisfying fantasy that she kept it running over and over, in the hopes that she would dream about it all night.

Then Roque dared to laugh. 'One touch from me and you would break up into hot little pieces.' His taunting drawl came across the pillow.

'In your dreams,' Angie mumbled.

'You never could resist me,' he insisted. 'You are like this iced-in little flame on the outside, but on the inside you've always been so hot for me it's like an extra pulse-beat, throbbing incessantly in your blood. I only have to look at you and you're dead meat, Angie. I am your sexual master—always have been.'

That self-promoting statement brought her lurching into a sitting position, pushing her tangled hair back from her face. 'Well, you conceited swine,' she heaved out. 'Do you really believe that you are the only man to ever make me feel like that?' She turned her head to look down at him through the darkness. 'You do, don't you?' She caught the mocking glint in his eyes. 'You genuinely believe that because you were my first lover I couldn't possibly want to make love with any other man. Well, I have news for you, Roque. I moved on—just like you did.'

The glinting eyes took on a dangerous aspect. Lying through her teeth had never come easy to Angie, but, gosh, it was worth it to see that glint.

'And you can quit looking at me like that,' she told him.

'Like what?' he questioned softly.

Angie felt a sudden need to anchor the duvet tight around her chest. 'Like I'm talking dirty,' she enlightened him, then added a scornful little laugh. 'Yet you're the one with the serial sexual record. No wonder you have such a bad playboy image. You earned it recording notches on your bedpost of which I was only one.'

'Is that so?' he breathed, barely distinctly.

In full aggrieved flow now, Angie nodded her tumbled head before throwing herself back against the pillow. 'Exclusive you are *not*.'

'So you decided to follow my example and take a few lovers or your own? Is that what you are telling me?'

Even through the darkness Angie could read the level of threat contained in his tone well enough to fling herself onto her side, as far away from him as she could get.

'I would need to be taking sex-enhancing drugs to follow *your* example.' She thumped her remaining pillow again and then resettled her head. 'All I'm saying is don't put yourself on a sexual pedestal of my making. I've been around now. I've known better and worse lovers than you, so—'

He moved so fast that even though she had been half expecting it he still drew a choky cry from her at the speed with which she found herself pinned flat on her back.

'Better than me?' he scythed out.

'Well…hello, Mr Ego,' Angie drawled as his angry breath warmed her face.

His glinting eyes narrowed. 'Tell me you are lying to me.'

Angie arched perfectly formed dusky brown eyebrows and said nothing.

'You are out for revenge. You are trying to score points.'

'Not finding it nice to have your prowess compared with others, *querido*?'

Roque shifted against her, and somehow managed to make her legs part enough to accommodate the pressure of his hips.

It was okay, Angie assured herself. The duvet was

between them. He still wasn't touching her skin. His
warmth seeped through the barrier, though, as did the
lurking evidence of his hard male potency pressing
against the soft apex of her legs. He was supporting his
weight on his forearms. Hard-muscled biceps shone in
the dimness, displaying a physical strength that echoed
the power built into his chest. And his long fingers hovered a small centimetre away from her cheeks, teasing
her with the threat of capturing her face, so the skin
there prickled and tingled in readiness.

And she was hot, feeling stifled by the duvet and by
the heat coming from him. Eyes as black as jet held onto
her defiant green ones, showing enough of a glitter to tell
her he was not at all happy with the way this particular
battle had taken shape. Now he was waiting for her to
say something else foolish, so he could react.

But what he really wanted her to do was to confess
that she'd been lying.

'You're heavy,' she told him.

'You love to feel my weight bearing down on you,'
he came back, soft as air. 'You like to feel overwhelmed
by me so you can have an excuse to let go of everything.
Did your other lovers not recognise this?'

Angie moistened her lips, dried by his warm breath,
and didn't answer.

'Frustrating for you, was it, *minha doce*, not having
your special needs catered for?' he goaded, shifting that
oh-so sexy mouth even closer to hers. 'In your desire to
knock me off my pedestal were you driven to closing
your eyes and opening your legs for these many new
lovers?'

'Don't be so disgusting,' she mumbled absently, engrossed in watching his lips move.

That wide, passionate mouth stretched. 'I could have you crawling all over me in seconds,' Roque taunted. 'Before you could draw in a single breath you would be making those soft, anxious whimpers of pleasure while you tasted me. Ice-cool Angie you were *not* in my bed, *querida*. You were a sexy, slinky, greedy little wanton with only one goal in mind: having me deep inside you and driving you out of your head.'

Angie's eyes were almost closed. She was trying so hard not to let his huskily delivered taunts spark a response from her. But her body was not playing. Her body was stirring up every sense she possessed.

As if he knew it, Roque shifted on her slightly, and the tips of her breasts stung as they sprang into tight, tingling pinpricks of feeling against the tautly stretched duvet. Gently but surely he pressed his hips downwards, and the greater contact with her thighs made them start to pulse. And still his fingers continued to hover a hair's breadth from her cheeks. Still his mouth maintained that tiny tantalising gap above hers.

'Come on, Angie, say something,' he encouraged. 'Describe how these many lovers matched up to me.'

Mutely, Angie shook her head.

Roque sucked some air. '*Were* there any other lovers?'

'You deserve there to have been a thousand other lovers!' she burst out, without knowing she was going to say it.

And that was it—the moment she lost it. The anguished force of her response sent her lips brushing against his, and sparks flew as the volcano of feeling burning inside her just blew its top. She dragged an arm free of the duvet so she could punch him. Roque muttered something as he ducked his head, then captured her mouth with a full-on, hot, driving kiss. With a whimper like those he had just described, Angie hit out at him again, and kept on hitting him—and kissed him back like a wild, reckless wanton.

But she was sobbing while she kissed him. She was writhing and gasping and still hating him. He crushed her into the mattress and scorched her with the ferocity of his own burning passion, until her hands went from punching him to clutching at his hair instead, her hot angry tongue spearing urgently between his lips.

Shattered by her own surrender, Angie found she could not contain what she'd let loose. It was as if twelve long months of grievous hurt just tumbled out of her. She felt wild with pleasure, and furiously angry at the same time. Hot, needle-sharp pricks of excitement set her fingers anxiously kneading his scalp. She could feel the heavy beat of his heart through the duvet and her limbs were melting. The thickness of his arousal was a blatant pleasure force he used to encourage her thighs even wider apart.

When he raised his head she found she was panting like a sprinter. His ridiculously dark eyes leapt with burning flames, his deep chest heaving, his teeth gleaming white in the darkness between his hot pulsing lips.

'Were there any other lovers?' he repeated the question.

Wanting that mouth back on her mouth—needing it there— 'No,' she squeezed out.

He threw himself away from her, rolling back across to the other side of the bed. Angie just lay there in a state of shocked numbness, stunned that he could just stop like that, but more appalled at how easily he had turned her into this shivering, quivering sensual wreck.

Then he really deepened her humiliation by picking up the pillow she'd shoved between them and repositioning her pathetic barrier as if it was himself he was trying protect now.

'Go to sleep,' he rasped, before he slid onto his side with his back towards her.

Angie rolled onto her side too, opening a gap between the two of them that made the silly barrier superfluous in a bed as big as this. Her eyes were burning with unshed tears, and she wondered if this was the point where she finally let them escape. She knew deep inside she had asked for everything Roque had just dealt out to her. She'd challenged his ego, poured scorn on his masculinity, and derided his prowess as a lover. Having satisfactorily reclaimed all three of those things, he was now content to fall asleep.

Taut as coiled wire, curled up in a ball, she pushed a hand up against her quivering lips and closed her eyes tightly, working very hard to make sure he did not feel the tremors shaking the bed. She would get up in a minute, she told herself. She would wait until the rotten, faithless, cruel brute had fallen asleep, then she would go back to the other bedroom and this time lock the door so he couldn't get in…

She dreamed of locked doors and the helpless constraints of imprisonment as if someone had locked her in. Anxious, restless, she had no idea that she was whispering little pleas into the darkness, begging to be set free. When she uttered a small sob, Roque gave up on lying there watching her, removed the pillow from between them, and gently drew her into the middle of the bed. She curled into him as if she was hunting for safety, and whispered his name against his throat.

Angie slept straight through until morning, when she came awake with a jittery start as if something or someone had woken her up. Remembering exactly where she was arrived half a second later, launching her into a sitting position as full recall of the night's events flooded into her head.

Pushing her hair back from her face, she swivelled a wary glance at the other side of the bed. It was empty. Relief quivered through her—followed by a burst of fury aimed entirely at herself, for falling asleep here when she'd meant to hot-foot it out of this bedroom and lock herself into the other one.

What time was it?

A glance at her watch sent her diving out of bed. She should have been walking into work as of *now*! Rushing out of the room and down the mezzanine landing to the other bedroom, she headed directly for the bathroom, and only thought about Roque's meeting with her brother when she was standing beneath the shower.

Had he already left?

Quickly drying herself, she grabbed the bathrobe hanging up behind the door and dragged it on as her bare feet took her back out onto the landing and down the stairs. Last night's dinner things had been cleared away, she saw as she crossed to the kitchen—then came to a thoroughly disconcerted halt.

A complete stranger stood elbow-deep in washing up suds—a long, tall, curvy-shaped stranger, with short floppy blonde hair, wearing jeans and bright pink sneakers to match her bright pink tight, stretchy top. When she turned around Angie saw she had big baby blue eyes and a lush heart-shaped mouth.

'Oh, good morning, Mrs de Calvhos.' The lush mouth broke into a melting smile. 'I'm Molly Stewart,' she introduced herself. 'I come in here each day to clean up.'

Roque employed a blonde bombshell as a daily cleaner? Suspicion as to Molly's real role here slunk like poison through Angie's blood. What had happened to old Mrs Grant?

'Do you know where my husband is?' Angie asked, stunned to hear herself use that possessive title as if she was sending out a warning to the blonde.

'He left about half an hour ago,' Molly Stewart told her. 'He said for me to let you sleep.' Picking up a towel, she began drying her hands on it. 'Can I get you some breakfast? Cereal and juice? Some toast and a pot of coffee or tea?'

'No—thank you,' Angie answered with polite cool. 'I'll—I'll just grab a bottle of water from the fridge.'

Why was she behaving so awfully? she asked herself. Because you don't like the thought of this sexy creature polishing Roque's floors and making his bed, Angie answered her own question, frowning as she crossed the kitchen towards the fridge, with the blonde watching her every step of the way.

It all felt just so weird—as if she was an intruder here. A one-night stand left behind to sort herself out while the great Latin lover disappeared out of the firing line of an awkward morning-after scene.

Then she wondered just how many one-night stands Molly the daily had greeted with offers of breakfast.

Had Molly Stewart been one of them? Was Roque into seducing the cleaning lady on her days off?

Not liking the ugly path her mind was taking her along, she tugged open the fridge door and selected a small bottle of water, then pushed the door shut again, turning to find Molly staring at her pensively, as if she had something she wanted to say.

'Your husband said I was to make sure you ate something, Mrs de Calvhos,' Molly murmured anxiously. 'In fact he was very specific—'

'That is not his decision to make,' Angie responded, with a snap she would have preferred had not been there. But she was struggling with hearing herself referred to as 'Mrs de Calvhos' now, because she didn't feel like a Mrs *anyone*. She didn't want to feel like a wife at all.

Especially so after last night's humiliating fiasco in Roque's bed.

Great will power you have, Angie, she thought grimly, then glanced up sharply as Molly suddenly rushed into speech.

'You're Angie Hastings, aren't you? Gosh, you're even more beautiful in the flesh than you look in the magazines.'

Thoroughly startled by this unexpected compliment, Angie just stared, and Molly started blushing as if she'd made some terrible gaffe. Angie suddenly saw how young she was—and actually kind of cute. Despite possessing the sexiest curves she'd seen in a long time, being in the industry Angie was in, Molly Stewart had a natural warmth about her that made Angie feel mean for being so cool with her.

'Let's start again,' she offered with a ruefully apologetic smile. 'I was surprised to find you here, and I'm cross with my…just cross,' she edited, unwilling to use that *husband* word again. 'I should have been at work by now, and—'

'I wish I had your hair,' Molly cut in breathlessly. 'The colour is fabulous…'

'Trust me, you don't.' Angie gave in and just laughed. 'It's hell to manage, and you can't hide the fact that you're a genuine ginger-head. Did my…?' There it was again—the word she didn't want to utter. Avoidance is futile, Angie, she told herself whimsically. 'Did my husband leave a message for me other than that I am supposed to eat?'

'Oh.' Molly jumped. 'He wrote you a note…' Walking across the kitchen, she picked up an envelope, then released a giggly laugh. 'He also said that if you tried to leave the apartment I was to barricade you in, but I don't think I was supposed to pass that detail on.'

Frowning again, because Angie was picking up on a definite air of friendly intimacy being passed around between Roque and Molly, she asked as casually as she could, 'How long have you worked here?'

'Since I started full-time at the London Business School, with the help of Mr de Calvhos's financial sponsorship,' Molly informed her with prompt honesty. 'I could not have studied full-time without his help, so I try to pay him back by keeping this apartment nice for him to come back to when he's in London… My grandmother used to work here before me, but she had to retire due to ill health.'

'Oh, I'm sorry. I hadn't heard that Mrs Grant was ill.'

'She's not any more.' Molly smiled as she handed an envelope to Angie. 'Mr de Calvhos paid for her to have private treatment and she's in fine health now. He's been very good to us. We are ever so grateful.'

Hating herself for wondering *how* grateful, Angie let the envelope claim her attention instead. Murmuring something about going back upstairs to dress, she took the envelope with her, and didn't open it until she was back in the guest bedroom.

'I have organised professionals to clear out your apartment, so I've taken the keys from your bag,' Roque had scrawled, without a care for the presumption he was displaying. 'Be sensible and don't try to contact your brother. Wait here for me. I will be back by lunch. R.'

Be good and stay put and wait for him like an obedient wife, in other words. Angie read between the lines of the final part of his missive, and instantly dived for her green bag, with the intention of fishing out her mobile phone to do exactly what he had told her *not* to do and call Alex.

It wasn't there.

He didn't trust her to do as he'd ordered, so he'd taken her phone as well as her keys!

Refusing—point-blank—to acknowledge that she had been about to add substance to his lack of trust in her, Angie stood seething with frustration for a few seconds. Then she remembered the time and took her frustration out on finding something to put on.

At least her holdall was still there, she saw. He hadn't gone as far as removing her clothes so she couldn't leave. Ten minutes later she was walking back down the stairs, looking hard-edged and street chic in drainpipe designer jeans and a purple top which should have clashed horribly with the green bag but somehow didn't. She'd scrunched her hair back from her face, and now wore a pair of high, chrome-heeled leather clogs on her feet.

Molly stared in awe at her as she strode towards the lobby. 'I wish I could look like that in ten minutes,' she sighed wistfully.

Try living and breathing the fashion industry for a few years, Angie thought ruefully. She'd learnt quickly that it was all in the execution.

She managed to grab a passing cab as she stepped out of the building. Fifteen minutes later she was striding into the glossy white reception area belong to CGM Management, ready to take up her duties a whole hour late, only to be met by the surprise sight of her employer calmly manning the front desk.

'You look as if you've spent a night on the tiles,' Carla Gail drawled by way of a greeting.

Carla was an ex-supermodel from the nineteen-eighties, still stunningly beautiful, with a long slender figure and wheat-blonde hair. Inside she was made out of cut crystal, with a business brain that scared most men into shivering shakes.

'Sorry I'm late,' Angie apologised, without bothering to respond to the critique. 'I overslept.'

'With anyone I know?' Carla posed curiously.

Angie lifted up her chin. 'You want me to publish a kiss and tell?'

'God, no,' her svelte blonde boss refused, 'Too boring, sweetie. And, knowing you as I do, it was probably the kid brother who put those worry bruises beneath your eyes. Get someone in Make-up to do something about them.'

Carla strode off then, leaving Angie to grimace at how close to the truth Carla's supposition had been.

A steady string of hopeful wannabe models arriving for interviews kept the morning busy. Angie was experienced enough to know at a glance which of them—if any—were going to be seen by someone higher than the lowliest ranking member of the team. She kept looking at her watch, wondering what Roque was saying to Alex. Several times she almost gave in and called her brother using the desk phone, but then someone else would walk through CGM's famous glass doors and the temptation would fade for another few minutes.

When lunchtime arrived, so did an increase in her stress levels. Had Roque arrived back at the apartment yet? Was he angry that she wasn't waiting for him there like a good girl? Had he murdered her brother, or just threatened to do it? Was Alex trying to call her on her mobile phone?

Carla strolled back into the foyer with a casual glide that said she was on her way out to lunch. She paused halfway across the shiny white foyer as her mobile phone leapt into life. Lucky Carla, Angie thought as her boss paused to speak to her caller, then flicked a strange glance at Angie before turning back the way she had come.

'Give me a minute to reach my office,' Angie heard her murmur as she strode by.

Business before food. Business before pleasure. That was Carla, Angie thought. Her personal life currently involved a low-ranking member of the British aristocracy who liked to keep his extra-marital affairs discreet. Which, when she thought about it, was why Carla had turned bored at the mention of kiss and tells. Carla would rather be boiled in oil than swap personal stuff with anyone. The only reason Angie knew about

Carla's lover was because she'd been having dinner at Carla's apartment one evening when the guy had turned up unexpectedly.

The hidden wheels and cogs of life, she mused cynically. She had yet to meet a married couple who could truly claim they had a strong, happy relationship—not in *her* social and business sphere anyway. Hotshot businessmen with vast wealth and huge responsibilities needed to vent their manic stress levels somewhere other than with the little wife.

She had watched it go on so many times during her modelling days. High-end mistresses attending catwalk shows with blank chequebooks provided by their indulgent lovers whose sadly blind wives would more often than not be at the self-same shows, with their own blank chequebook to use. It was the ugly underbelly of a beautiful world. A world she had vowed would never tempt her. Yet she'd fallen in love with and married such a man—a man who would turn into such a man when he got older, more jaded, and bored with playing happy families.

Had turned into one, Angie reminded herself, and he'd done it so fast that even she, with all her cynical views on marriage to rich men, had been left flailing like a landed fish, left to die a slow, suffocating death while the fisherman moved on to more appealing fishing grounds.

It wasn't the best bit of timing for CGM's plate glass doors to swing open and for Angie to glance up and see Roque striding in.

CHAPTER SIX

HE WAS wearing a grey pinstripe suit that draped his long, powerful frame as if it loved being there, and he looked—sensational. Tall, dark and tanned, with the kind of hard-angled, well-balanced features that just instinctively attracted women to him: the exotic curve of his cheekbones, the thin fleshless nose, the gorgeously sexy full, sensual mouth.

Her insides gave a telling little leap of soul-deep attraction, her eyes unwillingly gluing to the slightly sardonic gleam in his. And he was smiling.

But, worse than all of that put together, Angie could see him naked again, after his conceited pose beside the bed he had dumped her on last night. And this was a guy who liked snowboarding down the Alps or skydiving off them. This was a guy who swam umpteen laps of his swimming pool every day before breakfast and could pump iron without breaking into a sweat. So he had pecs, he had abs, he had big strong shoulders and bulging biceps, and a chest splashed with virile dark hair hidden beneath the fine cloth of his bright white shirt, and muscles that could take her breath away cording his long, powerful legs inside the smooth cloth of the pinstriped suit.

As he strode towards her a whole line of wannabes lost their boredom in favour of covetously lapping him up. Jealousy erupted. It was so horribly possessive Angie wanted to tell the wannabes to get their greedy eyes off him.

Mine, she heard some inner voice insist, and despised herself for feeling like that.

She shot to her feet. 'I want my keys and my phone back,' she hissed at Roque the moment he came to a stop at her desk. 'And if you've hurt my brother you are going to be sorry.'

The row of wannabes shifted on the shiny black leather chairs they were sitting on, their interest further piqued.

Roque lost his smile.

With the instincts of a natural-born predator cornering its spitting prey, he used his superior height to lean forward and stretch a long-fingered hand out across the desk to capture her chin.

'*Bom dia*, my beautiful green-eyed shrew,' he greeted her softly. 'May I advise you to keep your fight with me under wraps until we do not have an audience?'

The *shrew* part hit its mark, and Angie flushed. He was right. She was turning into a terrible shrew, all bitter and twisted and— 'You—'

He kissed her into silence. He just leant further across the width of her shiny black desktop and claimed her shrewish mouth.

A skitter of appreciatively amused gasps ran along the row of wannabes. Feeling the helpless softening of her lips, for a second Angie feared that she was going to start gasping too. By the time he drew away again her lips were warm and pulsing and her cheeks were on fire, and Roque was looking grimly satisfied because he'd felt her respond to him.

'Well, if this doesn't answer a lot of questions…' a cool voice drawled from somewhere just beyond Angie's hazy vision.

It was Carla, being as sardonic as she possibly could be.

'*Bom dia*, Carlina.' Straightening away from the desk, Roque greeted her smoothly, using Carla's full name even though he knew she disliked it. 'You look *atordoar*, as always.'

'I do hope that was a compliment, Roque,' Carla responded.

'What else?' Roque sent her one of his charismatic smiles.

Walking forward, Carla aimed a brief glance at the row of onlookers, which sent their heads dipping as if they'd been struck by a whip. Then Angie watched her boss hold out a hand for Roque to take.

It was only when Carla said, 'Shall we leave Angie to—cool down, and go through to my office?' that Angie realised with a start there was something happening here that she wasn't privy to.

'What—?'

'Ask Izzy to hold my calls, Angie,' the boss side of Carla interrupted what Angie had been about to say.

The two of them strode off, leaving Angie gaping after them. Roque didn't even spare her a second glance. It was obvious that Carla had been expecting him. More obvious now that the call Carla had taken here in the foyer a few minutes earlier must have been from Roque. She recalled the strange glance Carla had sent her before she'd walked back the way she had come.

And, whatever it was that Roque was up to now, Angie began to feel cornered. Was he sweet-talking Carla into sacking her? Was she about to become jobless as well as his reluctant wife again?

And what about her brother?

Making a quick decision which was really a surrender to something she'd been trying to stop herself from doing all morning, Angie picked up the desk phone and called her brother's mobile phone.

There was no answer. It didn't even go to voicemail. By the time Roque reappeared the wannabes had been led away into CGM's hallowed inner sanctum and Angie had turned from shrew into anxious-eyed mouse.

'Where is he, Roque?' She almost fell on him in her urgency to know the answer.

He caught her by her elbows. 'You called him?'

Angie nodded. 'He didn't answer.'

Something very close to grim satisfaction honed the naturally sensual curve of his mouth and Angie leapt on it. 'What have you done? Why isn't he answering his phone? Did you—?'

'Calm down,' Roque said, turning slightly, so she could see Carla standing just behind him, viewing their interaction through curious eyes. The last thing Roque needed right now was for Carla to jump back onto Angie's side of the fence after the work he'd just put in bringing her down on his side.

'*Adeus*, Carlina,' he bade her coolly, barely giving Angie time to snatch up her bag before he was ushering her towards the exit as fast as he could.

'I will expect to hear from you, Roque,' Carla fed after him like a threat.

'*Sim*. Soon,' he promised over his shoulder.

Outside the building, instead of his Porsche, a sleek chauffeur-driven silver limo idled on double yellow lines five strides away. Even with her long legs Angie struggled to keep up with him as he covered the distance in three. Handing her into the rear seat, he joined her and closed the door. A second later they were slipping smoothly into London's nose-to-nose traffic.

'What's going on?' Angie twisted on the seat to spear a taut look at him. 'What have you been discussing with Carla? Have you just lost me my job? And where is my brother? You had better come clean fast, Roque, because you won't enjoy watching me fall into a screaming rage!'

'You are already there.' Turning his dark head, he scanned her taut features and bright eyes. 'If you had invested this much emotional energy into trying to make our marriage work we would not be in this present situation,' he clipped out in contempt.

'Well, that's great, coming from the man who took other women to bed,' Angie flung back.

He removed his eyes from her and said not a single word in his defence, and Angie slumped back against the soft leather upholstery. 'You're such a hypocrite.'

'Your brother still has his head attached to his neck,' he drawled, as cool as ice. 'He is not languishing in a police cell or cowering in a dark corner somewhere, scared that I have set a band of hitmen onto him.'

'Thank you,' Angie murmured, with excruciatingly well-mannered ill grace.

Then she glanced back at him, to find he was looking at her again. The skin banding her throat started to prickle, because the way he was looking at her somehow relayed his resentment for needing to look. Sparks flew between them—they always did. Hot sparks, angry sparks, sexually stimulating, breath-catching sparks.

'What was all that with Carla?' Angie mulishly persisted when his mood told her she should not.

'Business.'

And that was it? The dark glint in his eyes dared her to continue. The need to constantly take him on fizzed like a fever in her blood. It had something to do with not letting him claim the upper hand over her, for he was the kind of man who would eat her alive if she gave him the chance.

The car pulled up outside his apartment block. Angie frowned when Roque instructed the driver that they would need him again in a couple of hours.

'Why? Where are you going?' Having to rush to keep up with him again, Angie was forced to ask the questions to his back.

He stabbed the lift button and leant back against the casing like a surly boy in a very bad mood. 'Just shut up for two minutes, Angie,' he growled at her. 'I am still too angry with you to want to play fair right now.'

Widening her eyes, 'What have I done?' she cried out.

He didn't bother to answer. He just strode out of the lift like a man in search of escape.

Angie followed at a slower pace, confused, really unsure of her ground now, for she did not understand his mood. Molly the cleaner was no longer in evidence, she noticed. Everywhere looked polished and neat. Sliding her bag off her shoulder and depositing it on one of the sofas, she followed Roque as he made directly for his study. The way he threw the door open wide made her blink in anticipation of it hitting the cabinet she knew stood just behind it.

It didn't hit the cabinet, but she was still left with a wincing sensation as if it had. This was crazy, she thought. She didn't even know what he was angry about! And what had he been discussing with Carla? Why had her boss let her go with him without putting up an objection?

Tugging in a deep breath, she followed him, determined to get some answers even if it felt as if she was about to enter the lion's den. And her heart was hammering at the prospect of taking him on yet again, she noticed.

He was standing behind the desk with his dark head lowered as he flipped through the small stack of mail Molly must have placed there. Angie could not see his face, but she could feel the circle of grim reserve he had drawn around himself like an invisible line he was silently warning her not to cross.

Pressing her teeth down into her bottom lip, she made herself walk forward. 'Roque—'

'Smile for me, Angie,' he said.

'Wh-what?' She pulled to a nerve-crunching standstill.

'Smile for me.' He lifted his head up and speared her with a grim, cynical look. 'I smiled for you when I came to collect you this lunchtime. So—smile for me. You owe me one. Smile for me and say something pleasant.'

This was a joke. It had to be a joke. 'You're angry with me because I didn't return your smile?'

'It is called interacting,' Roque provided. 'You know—man to woman—woman to man. I smile;

you smile back. I say *bom dia*, Angie, you say hello, Roque.'

'This is mad.' She threw her hands up. 'All I'm trying to do is—'

'If you ask about your brother just one more time...' he exploded, with quite spectacular force.

'I wasn't going to!' she lied, only to blush and spoil it. 'What's got into you, for goodness' sake?'

He responded with an action that stalled Angie's ability to draw air into her lungs. He opened the drawer and withdrew her chequebook, then tossed it down on the desk. As she watched in blank silence her mobile phone arrived next, which he dropped onto the chequebook, followed by her keys, which he withdrew from his trouser pocket.

'Take them,' he invited, then slammed the drawer shut.

Angie couldn't move. A deep chill of foreboding was settling over her. He was going to give up on her. He'd changed his mind because he was already fed up with her shrewish attitude. She could feel the change of heart bouncing off the grim hardness of his long, elegant stance.

'Roque...please...' She didn't even care that she sounded pleading.

'Please, Angie?' he quizzed cynically. 'Now, there is a word I don't often hear you speak. Tell me, are you begging for your brother's sake or for your own sake?'

'I just don't understand what's the matter with you!' she cried. 'I thought we had an—an agreement, but the way you're giving off so many confusing signals I no longer know what I'm supposed to think!'

His dark eyes flared on a snap of anger. 'You remind me that we have an agreement, yet you've already defaulted on your side of it by taking yourself off to a different bedroom to sleep, then sticking a pillow down the middle of the bed when I carried you back to ours!'

Angie stared at him in gaping disbelief. 'You're in this mood because I refused to give you sex?'

'I could have had the sex if I'd been inclined to take it, Angie,' he drawled in grim derision, reminding her that *she* had not been the one who'd wanted to stop last night. 'I am not that big a slave to my libido,' he denied, implying that maybe she was. 'I accept that we both need time to—adjust to being together again.'

'Really?' Angie folded her arms and speared a look at him. 'Perhaps the blonde bombshell I met in the kitchen this morning keeps your libido less slavelike these days?' she struck back. 'Because all I recall from the last time we lived together is you wanting it wherever and whenever you could get it, and turning into a growling nasty bear when I said no—like you're doing now.'

'You never said no,' he countered. 'You grabbed with both hands and whatever other greedy part of your anatomy you could grab me with. When I mentioned the bed thing—' he rolled a long-fingered hand '—I was merely trying to point out that you have been defaulting on our agreement from the moment we agreed it. And who is the blonde bombshell?' he demanded curiously.

Feeling slightly ashamed that she'd brought Molly Stewart into this just to score points—though she was still uncertain as to whether the new cleaner *did* have other special duties—Angie stepped up to the desk.

'Thanks for my stuff.' She gathered up keys, phone and chequebook, then turned to leave.

'Where do you think you are going?' he sighed out.

'To make myself scarce while you decide what the heck it is we're supposed to be fighting about.'

'Well, don't make yourself too scarce. We are due to fly to Portugal in a couple of hours.'

Angie froze, then swung back round again. 'Portugal?' she echoed, as if he'd named a different planet.

'I live there,' Roque reminded her.

'Yes, but…' The ground suddenly felt shaky beneath Angie's feet.

'My London offices usually see me only one week a month.'

'Yes.' She knew that too. 'But…'

Roque looked at her and waited, drawing her hesitation out as if it was stretched on wires while her mind ran through the string of objections she wanted to utter before she discarded them one by one in case she fed his weird mood.

'I thought…' She stopped yet again, and her lips quivered on a shaky intake of air. 'There's my job—'

'Already sorted. Carlina has given you an extended leave of absence.'

So that was what their cosy meeting for two had been all about. Roque had convinced Carla to let her go, probably using the 'giving their marriage a second chance' excuse, and Carla had let him convince her without asking Angie what she wanted to do.

'You are not my mistress, Angie,' he inserted into the steadily thickening silence, so coolly she almost missed the relevance of the prod. 'In general mistresses stay put in one place while wives travel.'

Nadia suddenly stood between them like a raven-haired apparition, with a very smug smile on her beautiful face. Nadia was as exotically Brazilian as Roque was hot-blooded Portuguese. They even spoke the same language, which meant they could converse with each without anyone around them knowing what they said.

And Nadia travelled… As Angie had once travelled… Nadia followed the fashion drum wherever it led her, and if that happened to be the same port of call Roque was in then so much the better—did he think she was dumb?

'Well, I don't travel any more,' she said.

'You will go where I say you will go.' Roque flatly countered that. 'I let you off the hook too much the last time we were together. I let you dictate where and when I was allowed to be with my own wife. This time you will do the compromising, *querida*—and remember, please, before you start yelling at me, that your brother's present situation is depending on your absolute acceptance of that.'

A ragged laugh was torn from Angie. 'I don't even know what his situation is, since you haven't bothered to tell me.'

Roque flicked out a grimace in acknowledgement of that.

'But if you think I'm going to just fly off to Portugal and leave Alex here alone to get into—' Belatedly realising what she'd been going to say, Angie choked the rest of that sentence back.

Too late, though, to stop Roque from finishing it. 'Alex will not be left alone here in England to get into more trouble for the simple reason he will not be in England at all.'

She was staring at him now, in the grip of total

stillness, so concentrated on what he was saying that she couldn't even draw in a breath.

'We went together to speak to his college dean this morning,' he went on to explain. 'Alex is taking a gap year from his studies, effective as of now.'

'S-so where is he going?' Angie breathed almost indistinctly.

'Brazil,' Roque relayed. 'To my ranch near Sao Paulo, to be exact.'

'Brazil...?' she whispered, as if he had not added the other details.

'He is going to learn all about ranching, cattle farming, living off the land—'

'Brazil?' Angie repeated one more time, her voice rising to a shrill pitch. 'You are sending my nineteen-year-old brother to the other end of the world for a whole year without my say-so?'

'Alex is over eighteen. He is allowed to make these decisions for himself.'

That wasn't the point. 'You mean it was your decision! What were his options—Brazil or a prison cell?'

'*Sim,*' he confirmed, without flickering a glossy black eyelash. 'He chose to work the next year, helping to pay back what he stole from me.'

The blunt use of the word *stole* had its effect on Angie, paling her face even further and closing up her throat. 'S-so where is he now?' she only just managed to utter.

'As of right now—?' With a smooth flick of a bright white shirt-cuff he exposed his gold wristwatch and gave his attention to it. 'Experiencing the comforts of first-class air travel somewhere over the Atlantic,' he answered. 'On his way to Sao Paulo...'

For a whole thirty seconds Angie couldn't seem to find a reaction. Pure shock was holding fast. She just stared at Roque, still standing there behind his desk like some lofty, unreachable lord and master, dark as the devil and cool as a long drink of iced water. He watched the emerald glow in her eyes slowly, slowly disappear, until the colour had turned pure bottomless black. Then she lowered her head to look down at her hands, still clutching her recovered possessions.

'You took my phone,' she mumbled.

Not understanding the relevance of the comment, Roque drew his eyebrows together in a frown.

She said it again, this time lifting those darkened eyes back to his. 'You took away my phone so I couldn't call him. You sent him away without allowing me to speak to him before he left… Why would you do that?'

For the first time since this had begun Roque's voice revealed a hint of roughness. 'I felt it would be easier on you if you had no input—'

'Easier on you, you mean.'

'Alex needs to face up to his responsibilities,' he persisted doggedly. 'He did this a lot faster believing that you were out of the loop.'

'You—you let him think I've turned my back on him?'

Roque released a sigh. 'Angie—we agreed that I would take control of your brother—'

'Just shut up about our stupid agreement!' She would have screeched all of that at him if her voice hadn't become muffled by the strangling blockage currently in control of her aching throat.

'We need a breathing space to work on our marriage

without your brother constantly tossing a spanner in the works!'

'But I don't *want* to work on our marriage!'

'Then why are you standing here?'

The hard challenge shimmered over the full length of her taut figure. He dared to stand there, seemingly expecting her to turn into the perfect amiable wife because he had taken control of her brother and her life?

'Why are you bothering to do this at all?' she fed right back at him.

Roque lowered his dark head. 'My family does not do divorce,' he answered smoothly.

Angie had to suck in a long hard breath to control the ever-pressing need to tumble into the kind of wild weeping jag she had not allowed herself to vent since—

No… Swallowing tautly, she told herself she was just not going to go there, staring down at the things clutched in her fingers and refusing to let them blur out of focus.

'So we must try harder to make a success of our marriage this time around…'

Still she made no response, but the telling sheen in her eyes held him captive. It was as if she was projecting an image of Nadia into the gap between them, and he let out a sigh.

'I want to try,' he added, in a roughened tone.

She blinked her long eyelashes and the sheen was gone—but not the hurt, he saw.

'To your standards or mine?' Without giving him a chance to answer that, she spun away from him. 'Just be clear, Roque, that the moment I stop caring about my brother will be the same moment you will lose control over me.'

She closed the door softly on her way out, making Roque wince as if she'd slammed it, then grimace because what she had said was true.

The complicated paradox of having a relationship with Angie, he mused ruefully. Her brother was always going to come first.

He raked out a laugh, wondering why he was giving himself all of this hassle when there were lots of women out there he could be enjoying a perfectly contented relationship with.

The answer was in the question. He did not want any other woman. He did not want perfect contentment in his life. He wanted a red-hot-tempered, red-haired shrew, with a fierce ability to love unconditionally—so long as your name was Alex, not Roque.

CHAPTER SEVEN

ROQUE turned the Range Rover in through the gates of the Quinta d'Agostinho, and drove into a tunnel of trees. Darkness swallowed them up in a moment, the spread of the car's headlights arcing eerily across the narrow strip of tarmac and into the surrounding undergrowth, washing the colour out of everything. The narrow driveway twisted and turned from there on, keeping them climbing steadily, as they had been doing since they'd left Lisbon behind.

For the *quinta* nestled in historic splendour on a lush green plateau near the peak of a forest-strewn hill. To see the house at all, unless from an eye-squinting far distance, you had to be in the air and flying over the top of his steep grey-tiled roofs.

As the tunnel of trees eventually thinned out, Angie shifted on her seat for the first time since they'd swapped Roque's plane for his sturdy four-wheel drive. She had visited this place only once before, which felt oddly unnatural now, when this was after all her husband's main home. Roque also owned an apartment in a beautifully converted sixteenth-century palace in the centre of Lisbon, which they'd used to use a lot. But this fabulous estate, with its rich dark forests and neatly tended formal gardens, was almost a stranger to her.

The last of the trees gave way to an elegant spread of sweeping lawns and flower-strewn shrubbery. Light suddenly bathed the car. As if inexorably drawn by it, Angie sat forward even further, to peer through the windscreen up at the house itself, standing within its own pool of welcoming warmth.

Lit for the master coming home, she thought, feeling breathless and vaguely threatened at the same time, though she did not understand why.

Great wealth, quintessential elegance and centuries of history stood right there, in the sugared apricot colour of its grand manor house walls. Angie glimpsed softly lit deep ground-floor terraces, and pretty arched upper balconies dressed in white-painted latticework, and the stone-built tower curving out from one corner as if stuck on as an afterthought. She caught a glimpse of the silky blue water in the swimming pool shimmering in its own beautifully tended bowl of a garden towards the far side of the house.

Then the car took a sweeping turn to the left, dipping them down and away from the front elevation towards the left-hand side of the house, where several open-arched, stone-columned garages came into view.

Roque stopped the car, switched off the engine and climbed out.

Angie stared balefully at his proud, handsome profile as he strode around the car bonnet on his way to open her door for her. He held out a hand to help her alight, which she accepted. They had been very polite to each other since they'd left London. Polite, distant, seemingly finally emptied of words.

She shivered as the cool evening air touched her skin, and still without saying a word Roque slid out of his jacket and dropped it onto her shoulders.

She supposed he was thinking she should have worn her coat, but when numb silence was the current order of things she didn't bother to say it out loud. She'd found a turquoise jersey shift dress lurking at the bottom of her holdall—one of those garments made of crease-free fabric that was so easy to pack—so she'd changed into it before they left and just stuffed everything else back into the bag—including her coat, along with her green bag.

Even in the mood she'd been in, not wanting to care about anything, the natural stylist in her could not let her walk around in a turquoise dress with a huge vivid green bag slung over her arm. So all those essentials women had to carry around with them everywhere they went now resided in a Harrods carrier bag she'd found at the bottom of a drawer. It now languished with the assortment of luggage that had appeared at this end of their flight.

'Your things,' Roque had deigned to offer in flat response to her puzzled frown.

Her 'things', all professionally gathered and packed into a brand new set of tan leather trunks and cases, were now stacked in the rear of the Range Rover. She had been moved, lock, stock and barrel, in other words. Evicted and expatriated with the swift efficiency of a man who was so at his best when he was in charge.

A little man wearing a white shirt and a soft black apron appeared like a magician at Roque's side, with a deferential bow and a smile. Turning his attention to the newcomer, Roque conversed with him for a minute or two, then turned back to Angie. '*Meu querida*, this is Antonio. He speaks no English, so please be kind.'

The *be kind* bit struck Angie like the plunge of knife. Why would she be anything else to any of the staff in Roque's employ? Did he really think that she was such a shrew she did not know how to behave herself? The idea that he did think that hurt.

Finding a smile, she offered it to Antonio with an outstretched hand. '*Boa tarde*, Antonio,' she greeted him, as warmly as she could.

'*Boa tarde, senhora.*' Antonio beamed a smile back at her, then went off into a rush of Portuguese which forced Angie to angle a helpless look up at Roque.

'He is welcoming you,' he explained.

'Oh.' She looked back at Antonio. 'I…thank you.'

'*Obrigado,*' Roque corrected.

'*Obrigado,*' Angie repeated obediently.

Antonio bowed again, before removing himself to the rear of the car, and she felt Roque's hand arrive in the centre of her back, lightly pressing her to walk towards the house. They entered it by a side entrance, but still the black and cream chequered floor and rich mahogany woodwork spoke of timeless elegance lovingly preserved. The house was more like an antique emporium. Nothing Angie rested her eyes on was less than a hundred years old. Walking down a long hallway with Roque a half-step behind her, she felt as if he grew in stature the further inward they were drawn.

Eventually the chequered floor opened out onto a vast crescent-shaped grand front entrance, with spectacular wood and marble twin staircases sweeping up the curving apricot-painted walls to the floor above.

A neatly dressed woman who to Angie looked

uncannily like Antonio awaited them. The resemblance was confirmed when Roque explained that this was Antonio's sister, Zetta. After he'd guided them through the same greeting ritual, he added a few brief instructions to Zetta.

It was only when his hand returned to the base of her spine to urge her towards the stairs that it began to hit Angie why they had come in through a side entrance.

Roque was making a very expressive point.

For the only other time he had brought her here had been as his new bride, and he had carried her in his arms through the front door. There had been no servants waiting to meet them, just the two of them and their soft laughter as he insisted on carrying all the way up the stairs.

This time there was to be no such romantic gesture— just a side entrance through which to gain access to the house, and the use of her own legs to carry her up the grand staircase. No soft laughter, no stolen kisses along the way.

Roque walked one step behind her and even the atmosphere felt cooler, making her tense fingers clutch the edges of his jacket more closely to her as she walked. And the silence between them grabbed at her heart and squeezed it. What had they lost? What had they done to all of that warm, soft, beautiful romantic love they'd brought into this house with them on their wedding night?

Reaching the point where the two stairways came together in a graceful sweep, Angie turned beneath the wide plaster archway which led through to the upper wings of the house. Without needing instruction she turned to the right, which led to the master apartments

in this huge many-bedroomed place. Any idea of trying
to escape to a different suite of rooms didn't even get
an airing this time. It seemed pretty pointless to try it
when she knew Roque would simply do what he'd done
in London and gather her up and bring her here.

Anyway, she was all out of fight, tired and depressed,
feeling hollowed out from the inside by old memories
she wished she didn't have.

As they reached the door that barred the way further,
Roque stepped forward to lean past her and do the polite
thing with the door.

For a second she felt his arm brush her shoulder. For
a second she felt his breath stir her hair. For a second
she felt her senses leap and then tighten when he made
a breath-catching pause. She could feel him wanting to
say something, could feel his gaze on her half-lowered
profile, as if he was willing her to turn her head and
look at him.

Was he remembering the same things she was remembering? Her heart gave that same aching squeeze
again, and the need to take a breath or suffocate in
the heavy airlessness of their shared tension acted as a
stimulus to a set of vibrations she wished she couldn't
feel.

Then he was pushing the door inwards and she was
free to move again, walking on legs that felt rubbery into
a huge, beautifully appointed bedroom, with four long
windows dressed in a bitter lemon-and-lime-coloured
heavy silk brocade which matched the cover thrown
over the huge central bed.

Angie didn't look at the bed. She didn't really focus
on anything. She just slipped Roque's jacket off her taut
shoulders and draped it over the back of a chair, then

kept on going across an expanse of wooden floor strewn with beautiful rugs. She only came to a halt when she reached one of the windows, though it was much too dark outside to see anything through it.

'Antonio will bring up your luggage shortly.' Roque spoke at last.

Angie nodded.

'And Zetta is preparing a light supper,' he pushed on, sounding like a super-polite hotel concierge. 'As the hour is so late, I thought you might prefer to eat it up here.'

Angie nodded again, then added a courteous, 'Thank you.'

The long hiss of his breath ran straight down her spine. 'Angie—'

'I'll have a bath first, if that's okay,' she interrupted.

'Of course it is okay.' He'd started to sound irritated, but she didn't react—didn't want to react. She didn't want to fight with him any more. She felt cold and empty, as if she'd lost something precious.

Which she had, she acknowledged bleakly. Her freedom of choice.

She could almost feel him biting back the desire to say something else, but instead he turned and strode back out of the suite, the door closing into its housing with such a numbing softness it made her flinch.

Turning around, she crossed the bedroom and stepped beneath one of the plaster archways which stood either side of the huge, deeply carved bed. The archway opened up into a spacious, custom-designed dressing room she could have fitted the whole of her London flat inside. She crossed the floor to where she remembered the bathroom was situated, and by the time she'd run a bath in the huge porcelain tub, and indulged herself by soaking in it for ages, she began to feel more human again.

Wrapped in the velvet-smooth white bathrobe she'd found hanging behind the door, Angie padded out of the bathroom—only to pull to a stop in surprise when she discovered that while she'd been soaking in the bath her things had been unpacked and put away. Her suits, her dresses, tops and blouses all hung in co-ordinated neatness in the open-plan-style wardrobe spaces. Her assortment of shoes lined up in rows. Toiletries, cosmetics, perfumes were all carefully arranged on the wall-to-wall mirrored dressing table, and everything else was either neatly folded away or placed discreetly in the central island bank of drawers.

I've well and truly been moved in, she noted ruefully. Then padded out into the bedroom to find the promised supper spread out on a table by one of the windows. She discovered fresh, warm crusty bread, a baby tureen filled with a light aromatic soup, and a pot of tea with the distinctive scent of her favoured Earl Grey.

Left alone to enjoy her supper, she eventually let her attention drift towards the bed. A bed she had carefully avoided looking at until now, because it was the place she had spent her wedding night.

A night of warm and gentle teasing, then wild and hot rising passion as their hunger for each other closed them in. She'd learnt right there in that bed that there was a difference between being a lover and being a wife, as if the vows they'd exchanged had cast aside the mere physical, opening them up to a new and deeper intimacy that had overwhelmed them both.

He had loved her then. Angie was sure of it. And she had so loved him. They'd told each other so over and over during the long, dark and deeply passionate night in that bed.

A bed she would share with Roque again tonight— and goodness alone knew what else he intended them to share. It had already been prepared, with the lemon and lime cover stripped away and left neatly folded on the ottoman at the end of the bed, the crisp white bedding turned down.

Well, hello, honeymoon, she thought with a mockery she did not like to hear at work in her head. But there it was, mocking her rather than the situation, because their real honeymoon had spanned only that one night before her mobile phone had started ringing and she'd been rushing out of here to catch a flight back to London. Her brother had got himself into trouble again.

It was a wonder Roque had put up with it, she thought now, almost eighteen months after the event. The thought made Angie rise up from the table, tense again suddenly, restless, not liking it that she was seeing how putting her brother's needs before everything, even their honeymoon, must have felt to Roque.

Like an interloper in his own marriage. Angie winced as she recalled Roque saying that. It was no wonder they'd stopped loving and started fighting.

The suite door suddenly swung open and Roque strode in, still wearing the dark suit he had changed into before they'd left London, minus the jacket, of course, and now also minus his tie. Butterflies inside her stirred into life. He oozed streamlined grace and smooth, dark sophistication, exotic and earthy and unconditionally male. The bright white of his shirt highlighted the width of this shoulders and long lean torso. The absolute finest dark silk-wool mix draped his hips, his long, powerful thighs and legs.

But when she looked at his face she could see the polite shutters were still in place, joined now by a grim purpose that put Angie warily on her guard as he strode up to her, then held out his hand.

Her eyelashes flickering slightly, she studied his closed features for a second, then looked down to see he was holding out his mobile phone.

'Take it,' he instructed.

Not understanding why she needed to, Angie moistened lips and did nothing.

'It is your brother,' he said. 'I managed to catch him between stopovers.'

It was ironic that he should do this now, when the last person she wanted to think about was Alex.

'Roque—' she said with a husky jerk, wanting—needing—to say something to him but with no clue as to what the something was.

The grim set of Roque's mouth moved in a tense twitch as he took hold of her hand and placed the phone in it, then turned and strode away again, crossing the room to disappear into the other dressing room. Angie followed his tall, straight, purposeful stride through slightly blurred and helplessly confused swimming eyes.

'Are you there, Angie?'

It was only as her brother's impatient voice arrived in her ear that she realised she'd lifted the phone to it. 'Y-yes,' she confirmed, blinking fast. 'I'm here. Are you all right?'

'Of course I'm all right,' Alex responded. 'What do you think I am—a baby?'

Yes, thought Angie. 'No, but…'

'I can't tell you how great all of this is,' he rushed on excitedly. 'I'm flying first class—'

'Wh-where are you?' Angie asked him.

'Hell, I don't know.' He didn't sound as if he cared. 'Some VIP transit lounge somewhere. I didn't register where. We stopped to refuel. Did you know you can have a shower and a massage while you wait in these places? Just great how the other half live.'

'But—what about your studies, Alex? You can't just—'

'Oh, blow my studies,' he dismissed with absolute indifference. 'I can return to them any time. This is just the very best thing that's ever happened to me, Angie. Roque's been amazing. Who would've thought it of the guy? Did he tell you I'm going to ride with real gauchos and learn to rope cattle and stuff? I feel really guilty now for being such a bastard to him.'

The line crackled, and Angie heard her brother mutter something. 'I didn't catch that,' she said, squeezing the phone closer to her ear.

'I've got to go. We're being called to board. Listen to me, Angie,' he went on quickly, 'I'm sorry I messed everything up for you two.'

'You didn't—'

'Of course I did,' Alex sighed out. 'I meant to do it! I was so jealous of him I wanted to split the two of you up. But taking that money was way too low. I'm lucky I've still got my head attached to my neck.'

'Alex—'

'I just want to say I love you, sis, but it's time I started taking responsibility for myself.' The line crackled again, and kept on crackling. 'I'm fine…' she thought she heard between the crackles. 'Do yourself a favour... Roque...'

'Alex—?'

The crackles stopped and the line was dead. Angie stood there, staring at the phone clutched in her tense fingers. Her brother was enjoying himself. He was excited. And suddenly Roque had gone from being his most hated enemy to his absolute very best friend. He didn't mind being shipped off to the other end of the world, away from her. In fact he sounded happy to be given the space!

A sob broke from her. She didn't know where it came from. A set of long fingers arrived to gently prise the phone free from her grasp. And she was trembling, Angie realised, quivering and shaking, with tears rolling down her cheeks.

'Take a couple of deep breaths,' Roque advised quietly.

But Angie shook her head. She wanted to cry. Now that she had given in to it, she wanted to sob her silly aching heart out.

'You're suddenly his hero,' she said, on a choke that could not make its mind up whether to be a sob or a laugh.

She'd stood between the two of them like a boxing referee, with arms outstretched to hold them apart while they'd thrown verbal punches at each other. Now, out of nowhere, they'd decided to call a truce. Why couldn't they have tried to do it when it would have meant something to her?

Now Nadia stood between her and Roque like a smug, smiling spectre. And not just Nadia, she thought as she broke down on another sob.

She heard Roque release a sigh, then his arms came around her. There was a stiff reluctance in the way he drew her close. They were still at loggerheads, she remembered. Allowing her contact with her brother had not been done in the form of an olive branch.

'I apologise,' Roque said, and even that left him with distinct unwillingness. 'I accept I should not have withheld your right to reassure yourself that your brother was okay before he flew off. But he was already in the air and I knew I could not contact him for hours. I am a ruthless bastard when I go after something,' he ended flatly.

'I can't make my mind up if you've sent him to Brazil to make a man out of him or because you just want to put him as far away from you as you possibly can.'

'A bit of both,' Roque confessed with a dry slice of honesty. 'Here—use this…'

He handed her a clean napkin off the table. Taking it from him, Angie took the hint that she'd cried enough tears and made an effort to put a stop to them. 'It's me who should be saying sorry,' she mumbled into the napkin. 'I didn't mean to fall to pieces.'

'If you want my opinion it is something you should have done a long time ago.'

He was probably right. For hours, days, months—years—she'd been bottling it all up without knowing she was doing it. From the age of seventeen she had lived her life by walking a narrow path wearing blinkers on her emotions, because it was the only way she had been able to cope. Survival had been everything—her survival, her brother's survival. Constant fear had dogged her every decision. If she got it wrong and could no longer afford to keep Alex safe in his private boarding school she'd risked him being taken away from her and placed in a state home or fostered out.

Then Roque had come along—a dangerously tempting diversion.

'You were right,' she sniffed into the napkin. 'I should not have let Alex run my life for me. I should've listened when you offered me advice.'

'Was that a concession?'

If it was, he didn't sound very impressed by it.

'It is late. I need a shower. Go to bed.'

Letting her go, he swung away from her to stride back across the bedroom, all arrogant distance and touch-me-not-with-your-concession cool.

'You think you're so perfect, don't you, Roque?' Angie flung after him shakily. 'You think that because all your predictions about my brother have come true it gives you the right to take the lofty high ground. Well, I have news for you,' she said as he stopped dead. 'You were no better behaved than Alex was when it came to wanting your own way. Alex was jealous of you. What was *your* excuse for turning our marriage into a battle in which only one of you could make me dance to their tune? Which one of you was the adult?'

His shoulders flexed inside his white shirt as her final stab sank deep. 'Poor Angie,' he struck back. 'Beaten into meek submission by her warring men.'

His derision washed angry colour into her cheeks, for she had never let anyone beat her into submission—especially not Roque. 'I made mistakes,' she admitted. How could she not admit it when she'd just stood here in the room and faced them? 'I was a lousy wife to you—'

'So you were,' he agreed.

Angie sucked in a painful breath 'Well, at least I didn't go looking for comfort in another man's bed!' she hit back with shaking fervour.

Roque swung around to look at her. A sudden stark look Angie read as remorse had taken hold of his lean golden features, and her breath stalled in her throat when he opened his mouth to speak.

'Don't you dare apologise,' she heaved out shakily.

Surprise made him blink. 'I had no intention of apologising,' he stated coolly. 'Why would I, when you have just said that you were a lousy wife?'

Angie wanted to throw something at him. Instead she had to make do with clenching her hands into two tense fists, because he was already striding with laconic grace into his own dressing room, leaving her standing there feeling...

She didn't know what she was feeling, she realised as she released her pent-up breath. He tied her in knots. He'd always tied her in knots. Was he expecting *her* to apologise for driving him into another woman's bed?

A gentle knock sounding on the suite door made her hurriedly relax her taut posture before she called a polite, 'Come in.' The door opened and a little dark-haired maid dressed in pale blue stepped in. She smiled shyly at Angie and indicated she'd come to collect the supper things. Angie smiled back, managed to discover the maid's name was Maria, and after thanking her wandered into the bathroom to use up some time cleaning her teeth and brushing the damp tangles out of her hair.

When she glanced into the mirror she saw a triangular face with wide-spaced green eyes, a thin little nose and a full, soft bow-shaped mouth. A mouth that was trembling pathetically, and eyes that had darkened with hurt.

Did he truly believe he could justify what he'd done by piling the blame on to her? Obviously he did, or he would not have said it—which did not bode well for the next scene they were about the share when they climbed into that bed out there.

She turned to slump back against the washbowl, staring down dully at her bare feet, because she knew that sleep was not on Roque's agenda this time. He'd let her off the hook last night, but there was little chance he was going to do so again. And the default charge he'd laid on her this afternoon was still stinging—because, God help her, she knew she was in danger of defaulting again.

Walking back out into the dressing room, she started hunting through drawers, looking for her nightwear. Finding the right drawer in a wide column of them, she was about to pluck out a slip nightdress when she spied another nightdress folded beneath it, and a sudden light of defiance lit her up.

Throwing off her bathrobe, she let it drop to the floor, then pulled the garment out of the drawer to shake out its voluminous folds. It was a real passion-killer—a long, loose thing that would cover her from neck to feet. It had been given to her by a lingerie company aiming to reproduce the pre-Raphaelite look for its ads. She even had a copy of the photograph in her portfolio. All the other models in the picture were wearing the very latest in sensationally sexy lingerie. However, as a contrast, she'd got to look the perfect picture of pre-Raphaelite virginal white modesty because of her flowing red hair and her ability to look pale and—

'Angie, we need to talk—*meu Dues*.'

A sharp gasp of air left Angie's lungs as she spun around, then froze. Roque was standing in the opening which led back into the bedroom, his full attention locked onto her with the stunning power of a magnetic force field. Angie lost the ability to breathe at all—for he might be looking at her as if she'd just popped naked out of a birthday cake, but she could not take her eyes off *him*.

He was wearing a towel wrapped like a sarong around his hips and nothing else. The towel might reach down to his calf muscles, but it didn't stop him from looking mind-stoppingly physically gorgeous. His hair was still wet, and beads of moisture clung to his wide bronze muscled shoulders, the spread of hair on his chest. A slow, thick lethargy began creeping over her. There was no way to avoid admitting it. Looking at Roque meant looking at pure male perfection, with a horrendous amount of raw sexual promise thrown in. Her eyes felt glued to the long, sleek form of his very masculine torso, bearing the kind of muscular ridges that ignited a series of familiar stings and prickles which attacked low down in her abdomen and at the very tips of her breasts. It didn't help that she knew him, every fabulous lean, dark, intimate inch of him, knew exactly what was hidden beneath the towel and what—

'*Meu Dues*,' he said again. 'I am revisiting my perfect moment.'

Angie blinked, then jerked her eyes back to his face. Roque watched as a blush started crawling across her skin as his meaning struck home. Seeing her naked for the first time was a moment he would treasure for the rest of his life. Her shy blushing cheeks, the soft quiver of her mouth, the rippling waves of her hair falling around her face and her shoulders, the smooth flowing lines of all that amazing pearlescent skin. The way she'd stood in front of him, with her thighs pressed anxiously together and her arms crossed over her body in a manner supposed to be hiding her breasts from him. But the two perfect globes had pouted at him over the top of her inadequate cover-up.

Back then he'd felt like the rake in some costume melodrama, about to deflower the pale trembling virgin, and he'd loved it. His Portuguese blood had fired up centuries of alpha genes which he really should have been ashamed to acknowledge he had. If his great-great grandfather had been alive to witness such primitive rushes he would have been pleased. Drogo de Calvhos had been a sixty-four-year-old lech and a childless widower when he'd married the sixteen-year-old daughter of a *duc*, sold to him for the price of some disputed land bordering their two estates. Fable had it that his teenage bride had put a scar on his face, trying to fight him off on her wedding night, and his ancestor had had her whipped for her trouble. She'd given him three sons before she'd reached her twentieth birthday, and each conception had added another scar to Drogo's face.

'Go away,' gasped Angie, casting the nightdress aside in favour of stooping down to snatch up her discarded bathrobe.

For some reason he could not fathom, Roque lifted a hand to lightly stroke the side of his cheek. Perhaps it was those genes at work again, warning him that he could receive the same treatment as his ancestor if he did not tread carefully around Angie right now. He might be only thirty-two years old, not sixty-four, and this woman a now very experienced twenty-three, but the vibes were still there—the *touch me if you dare* warning buzzing in the space separating them.

'Sweet heaven,' he breathed, 'you have gained curves.'

He started moving towards her, the burning heat in his dark gaze putting Angie into a panic as she fought to pull on the robe—only to discover that the sleeves had somehow become twisted inside out.

'It's a bit late for that, *meu amante*.' Reaching out to take the tangled robe from her scrambling fingers, he dropped it back to the floor.

Angie squeezed her naked thighs together and wished every hair follicle down there wasn't tingling like mad. He was standing so close to her she could feel the warm damp heat coming off him, smell the clean sharpness of his soap.

'You—you said you wanted to talk,' she reminded him, stretching out a hand towards the voluminous nightdress.

Roque caught the hand and brought it up to his mouth. 'I don't remember.'

'W-well you did—and stop that.' She pulled her hand free. 'I n-need to…'

She lost track of what she had been going to say when he took a step closer. Instinct sent Angie falling back a step, and she came up against the drawer unit with a bump. Roque just continued to follow her, with the unremitting certainty of a man who knew exactly what was going to happen next. One of his hands lifted up, open-palmed, with long brown fingers aiming purposefully for the indentation of her waist. When he touched her skin she quivered, and he smiled and just kept on coming, until his hips came to settle against hers.

'Roque…' she said, meaning to follow it up with a protest, but he got in first. Low, dark and somber.

'*Sim, minha dolce*, it is I.'

He sounded so grim again suddenly that Angie forgot to protest and frowned up at him instead. 'You—you're still angry with me,' she murmured unevenly.

'I am not angry with you.'

He showed her with the nudge of his hips exactly what he was. The towel folded around his hips was damp, but it did not detract from the burgeoning force Angie could feel making itself felt. Releasing a soft gasp was all she had time to do before he lowered his dark head and captured her mouth, beginning to explore it with a slow, deep, coaxing sensuality. His other hand arrived at her shoulder, gently urging her forward until their upper bodies met.

Trying to fight the kiss, the bold nudge of his erection, and now the feel of her breasts pressing against his warm skin, Angie pulled her head back and looked into the smouldering depths of his eyes. No matter what he'd said, he *was* still angry, she saw. Frowning, she parted her lips to say so, but he just drove his tongue between the gap, and followed it up with the hungry pressure of his mouth.

With a helpless groan she squirmed against him, trying to fight the helpless meltdown she could feel taking place inside. His long fingers spanned her narrow waistline. He used them to press her up against him. He kissed her until her lips were hot and swollen, and he felt her meltdown start to show itself in the slackening of her tension.

'Tell me you want me,' he instructed, seducing her heated lips with the words.

Angie folded her fingernails into the solid satin bulge of his biceps and pushed, trying to give herself some space.

'I *will* make you say it,' he warned, when she snapped her lips shut.

'You won't,' she responded unsteadily, staring with defiance into the burning dark certainty blazing from his eyes.

Raising a hand to clasp her nape, he tilted her head back, then with a precision that set her gasping bent his dark head and closed his mouth over one small, firm pointed breast. A hot stab of pure sensation spun down the front of her body, and she released a wild choking gasp. Her fingernails dug deeper into his skin so she could maintain her balance as raw, unbridled pleasure lost her the will to put up more of a fight. Her defences crashed and burned on a swirling eddy of thick hot craving. She groaned out his name, then lifted her hips into fierce contact with his. She felt his heartbeat quicken, felt the intoxicating throb of pure male muscle swell and harden at the contact.

She wanted him. Angie finally admitted it. She wanted *this*—Roque standing over her, making her feel small and delicate and fragile with his all-encompassing superiority in height, his strength, his everything. Her fingers left his arms to graze over his taut satin shoulders, and eventually curled into his wet, clean-scented scalp so she could lift up his head.

Their eyes clashed for a split second—his lit by flames, hers alive with emerald lights. She was panting. He looked ferociously turned on.

'Yes,' she said, that was all, and he claimed her waiting mouth.

She kissed him back with the same heated urgency, clinging to him as he ran his hands down her body, shaping her ribcage, the indentation of her waist and the swell of her hips. When the towel disappeared she arched towards him with the instincts of a wanton, going in search of contact with the fierce glory of his erection. The breath left his mouth on a silken hiss and he clamped a hand around one of her thighs and lifted it, arrogant in the way he wrapped it around his waist.

He was going to take her right here up against the drawers, with no preliminaries, and she wanted him to. She didn't need preliminaries. She was so ready for him, and it was like Roque had described it—an extra pulse beat through her blood. She wanted him to lose his head and sink himself into her to the hilt.

And he knew it too. She could see the knowledge in his eyes as he drew back from the kiss to look at her. He hovered, proud against her, hot and hard, looking down at her, allowing her to press soft, urgent, needy kisses to his lips and his face.

'Say it.'

Angie released a strangled laugh, because it was crazy that he still needed to hear her say it when she was already close to coming in a shivering, quivering, static-spangled rush.

Tightening her grip on his head, she pulled his mouth down onto hers with a hungry and hot sensuous passion that should give him his answer.

Muttering something deep in his throat, he took charge of the kiss—and of Angie. He lifted her up and wrapped her other leg around him, then carried her into the bedroom and to the bed.

Her hands became restless on his body—searching, greedy. When he started teasing her with slow moist kisses to her eyes, her nose, the sensitive hollows beneath her ears, she curled in closer in such a needy way that he uttered a mocking husky laugh.

Then he speared his fingers into her hair and bent his dark head to claim her mouth again, exalted by the grateful little whimper that rolled around her throat. *Mine*, he thought with simmering triumph, even if she did not want to be his. And with a long, smooth, possessive stroke of his hand along her body he made her quiver and writhe.

As if she knew what he'd been thinking, she said, 'I hate it that you can do this to me!'

'And I love it that I can do this to you,' Roque came right back.

Then he transferred his kisses to her neck, the swelling slopes of her breasts, and Angie forgot what they were talking about because she knew what was coming. She just clung to him, and the wait was unbearable as he plied hot, moist, grazing kisses over every inch of her flesh. His hands caressed where his lips were not reaching, layering sensation over sensation with the clever use of his hands and his mouth. When he finally gave her what she was craving for and dipped a finger between her thighs she just went completely still.

Roque lifted his head to watch the glaze of desire swim across the sensual glow of her eyes and see her breathing slow right down. His own heated response flooded his bloodstream as her silken wetness enfolded his touch. He reached up to touch his lips to hers, and she raised long and dusky eyelashes so she could look at him in trancelike sensuality.

'You love this, hmm, *querida*?' he husked.

She could not find the voice to reply. She just lifted up her fingers to trace his exotic cheekbones, warmed by desire. He was so beautiful to look at her heart ached. The fingertip delicacy of his touch was so instinctively perfect she experienced its pleasure through every pore. When he lowered his head to kiss her again she melted into it in the same luxurious way she had melted elsewhere.

It didn't stay like that for long, though. Like the beautiful calm before the raging storm, he wanted more—and he knew how to extract it. His kisses grew more demanding, his caressing fingers extracting a taut restlessness from her that set her panting and needing more. Her hands were moving all over him, touching, stroking, reclaiming each ripple of pleasure he experienced, each low, dark, husky groan. He bent to suck her tight aching breasts, and she closed the long thick power of his erection in both of her hands. It swelled for her, pulsing like a separate living thing, nudging her hip and demanding more from her—which she gave. And she felt the fluttering quickening in her body, felt her senses come alive in a vibrant rush that brought them tingling to the surface of her skin. Their mouths became a hot fuse of hunger again and again and again, until she could stand it no longer,

'Roque,' she breathed desperately. 'Please...'

He reclaimed her mouth with the silken fire of his darting tongue, and continued to trace the hot, vulnerable flesh between her thighs, dipping inside her, then frustratingly out again, finding and stimulating the tiny hidden nub and circling it until she flailed in a storm of excited frustration. He sucked her nipples with a ruthlessly determined urgency that had her fingers releasing him to clutch his hair, where they stayed, helpless and useless other than to cling, because her brain and her senses were being consumed in other places.

'Please, Roque, please…' she heard herself begging in a thick, tight, anxious little voice. Then, 'Oh…' She arched her spine at a streak of glorious pleasure. 'Do that again…'

He did do it again, and again, driving her into that white-hot mindless place where only his touch mattered. The heat of his breath was on her skin, and the dark rasp of words muttered in his own language as he urged her towards that agonised peak and almost right over it. Then, with the timing of an absolute master, he came over her and took her flailing over that peak with his first long, driving stroke.

It was like coming alive after a year lost in limbo. Angie came all around him in tense, hot rippling waves that increased in power with each plunge. He was hot and hard and increasingly urgent. He kept kissing her mouth, then her throat, then her shoulder, driving her crazy, because each heated touch was like a torment that did not last long enough.

He pushed the hair back from her face and commanded, 'Open your eyes.'

Angie obeyed without a single thought that he meant anything more than to add yet another dimension to what was happening between them. Breathless, panting, eyes dark green pools of desire, she looked into his deep dark gaze and saw the flickering flames of anger a split second before he rasped harshly, 'Say farewell to your fine moral principles, Angie.' And with a final long, plundering stroke tossed her, shocked, confused, shatteringly bewildered, into the spinning world of ecstatic release.

Afterwards she felt as if she was dropping down from a very high place onto stony ground. Her body still throbbed all around him. The power of her release still sounded like a scream in her head. Roque was heavy on top of her, and the evidence that he was taking this long to find his breath was a small kind of comfort to the way he had just deliberately demolished her.

She wanted to move, but she did not want to prompt him into saying anything else. *Say farewell to your fine moral principles, Angie…* That had been a big enough bludgeon to beat her with. She'd vowed she wouldn't have sex with him, now she'd done it, and Roque had wanted to make sure that she *knew* she had done it.

He moved finally, lifting himself up on his forearms and raising his head from the warm damp hollow of her throat. He looked at her. She looked at him. Nothing— not even a glimmer of emotion passed between the two of them.

Then, with a grimace, he slid off her—and the moment he did so Angie snaked off the bed. Tears were threatening, but she refused to give in to them. She tried her best to walk in a straight line towards the archway which led into her dressing room and bathroom, but she felt so light-headed and dizzy she was afraid her legs were going to buckle beneath her.

'*Retribuição,*' he fed after her impassively. 'It means retribution,' he enlightened. '*My* retribution. I did not sleep with Nadia.'

CHAPTER EIGHT

ANGIE stilled like a frozen icicle topped by a flaming river of fire.

'The tabloids misinterpreted what they saw,' he extended in a cold, flat voice. 'So you owe me, Angie, for twelve lousy months of being labelled a faithless playboy husband. Now you will never know what I've been doing and who I've been doing it with since you walked out on me.'

'So that—just now—was your idea of revenge?' she said without turning.

'I felt I was due something.'

Angie nodded her flame-bright head. 'Then I hope it gave you…satisfaction,' she murmured, and started walking again.

'Is that all you've got to say?' He sounded so sardonic she almost turned and ran back across the room to give him what he really should be getting—which was a slap across his heartless face! But she didn't. She was too hurt and cold and—worse than both of those things— too revolted with herself for giving in to him in the first place.

'As you said to me yesterday, this is a different time and a different set of issues. I thought we were trying to rebuild something here—not trying to demolish it completely. Silly me.' She even managed a laugh, albeit a bitter one. 'I should have remembered your ruthless streak.'

'Did you hear what I said?' He sounded irritated now. 'I did *not* sleep with Nadia.'

Angie breathed short and tensely. 'Does *she* know that?'

She started walking again, and actually managed to reach the opening archway before he spoke. 'You still don't believe me about Nadia.'

It wasn't a question. Reluctant though she was to do it, Angie turned to look at him, and was surprised to discover that he'd moved without her hearing him, and now stood in the opening to his own dressing room. It felt kind of ironic that they both stood naked, with the rumpled spread of the bed between them giving evidence of what they had just shared. For they might as well both be fully dressed and facing each other across a courtroom she felt so coldly indifferent to him now.

'I liked you better when you did not resort to lying to shore up your bruised ego,' she told him. 'I saw you, you see—with my own eyes. So coming up with such a weak story now is just a bit sickening to me.'

She should have walked away then, because it had been such a good exit line, but she didn't move. She stayed to watch the frown darken his hard, handsome face.

'You cannot have seen what did not happen.'

Well, she had. 'I came back that night,' she enlightened him. 'I got halfway to Alex's school, then changed my mind. I realised you were right. I had to stop putting him first and start thinking about us. So I got my driver to turn around and bring me back to London—to the club...'

She could still see it all, as if it had happened yesterday. Still feel the same clutch of anxiety as she'd stepped into the nightclub. It had been a friend of Roque's birthday. He'd invited a whole group of them to help him celebrate it. Julian someone-or-other—she couldn't recall the rest of his name right now. Not that it mattered.

'I saw you with Nadia.'

He'd gone so still now Angie wondered if he had stopped breathing. She certainly had, but there was nothing unusual in that for her when she allowed herself to recall the scene that had murdered her marriage. And by his taut silence she knew Roque was right there with her, seeing what she must have seen then. The tiny low-lit dance floor. The slow smoochy dance. Nadia with her arms wrapped around his neck, swaying against him. Roque using his hands to hold her close.

'She was all over you, and you were loving it.'

'No.' He denied that.

'You were loving it, Roque! Do you think I can't tell when you're aroused?'

'I was not aroused!'

'You were kissing her!' Angie was charged up like a stoked fire. 'Your hands were clamped to her backside! I watched the pair of you sway to the music and I would have to be really stupid not to know you were *both* only half a step away from having sex on the bloody dance floor!'

'Don't swear,' he growled, frowning fiercely now.

'I saved myself the indignity of being noticed and got out of there as fast as I could!' Angie careered on. 'I went to Carla's and stayed there the night. She woke me the next morning with a stack of tabloids showing you and Nadia *still* wrapped around each other, entering her apartment block!'

'She was drunk.'

Angie sucked in a fire-eating breath of air.

'I did not have sex with her—'

'Don't lie!' she yelled at the top of her voice.

'She was drunk—high on something anyway!' he fired right back at her. 'I took her home and dumped her safely inside her apartment. Then—I—left!' he punched out like a violent fist. 'I went *home* and sat up all night, waiting for my *wife* to come home!'

If Angie thought *she* was angry fit to burst, Roque had now hit the same furious place.

'But you did not come back. So I started ringing people! Your brother's school had not seen you. Carla told me that *she* had not seen you!' He threw out an arm in disgust. 'How damn cruel was that? She knew we'd had a row because I told her! I was *worried* about you! Then the newspapers happened. But *still* I trusted you to come home to me, Angie. To give me a chance to explain myself! You denied me that right! You judged and condemned me without a damn hearing, then flounced off out of the firing line for months without anyone knowing where you had gone. So I deserved my moment of retribution, *minha esposa*,' he insisted harshly. 'And you know what? The way you are standing there, willing to listen to me now, infuriates me even more—because it has come twelve months too late!'

On that final stinging volley he strode into his dressing room. Ten seconds later Angie blinked as she heard his bathroom door slam shut.

Pushing her tangled hair back from her face with

trembling fingers, she let a choky shrill laugh break free from her throat.

They'd just had their fiercest row yet while standing there stark naked. How crazily bizarre was that?

Reeling around, she walked into her own dressing room. Then, because anger was still fizzing around inside her, she walked into her bathroom and slammed *her* door shut.

Was he telling her the truth? *Could* he be telling the truth?

No, she refused to believe it—could not dare to believe it. Because it would make her hidden months of misery such a cruel, hard waste.

She was about to step beneath the shower when she realised she didn't want one. Like someone struggling to stay riding on the crest of a storm tossed wave, she reeled around yet again and went back the way she had come.

The bed looked like a war zone, and for some hazy reason she set about remaking it while her thoughts and her feelings tumbled around her insides.

Then she stopped.

Well, where *were* your fine moral principles, Angie? she asked herself suddenly. You just let him make hot, passionate love to you in this very bed when you still believed that he'd cheated on you.

Her prowling restlessness sent her back into the dressing room, where she saw her bathrobe and Roque's towel lying in a snowy-white heap on the polished wood floor. Stooping to pick them up, she straightened, hugging the towelling to her and instantly inhaling the scent of Roque's soap. Tears started to push at the muscles in her throat.

If he'd been telling her the truth then he *had* deserved his moment of retribution, she forced herself to acknowledge.

And she'd deserved to be on the cruel end of it.

Twelve long, lonely months that need not have—

Then she suddenly remembered something that stopped that train of thought abruptly in its tracks.

Who the heck did he think he was trying to kid here?

Spinning around in a full circle, she scanned the room looking for where whoever had unpacked for her had placed her Harrods bag. She couldn't see it. Frustration rose up to mix with the hurt and anger already foaming in her blood. Dropping the robe and towel, she made for the nearest hanging space and dragged a long black jumper off its hanger, yanked it on over her head.

Roque was just coming out of his bathroom when she arrived in the opening, a fresh towel wrapped around his hips. He saw her and froze.

'I want to know where my bag is,' she said.

The on the face of it harmless request made him blink. Roque stared at her for a couple of seconds—at the way she was standing there in a baggy black sweater that reached halfway down her fabulous long legs, at the way she'd folded her arms across her front—before lifting his eyes to view the way her eyes were sparking green ice at him. He was glad he was wearing a towel to hide what his reaction was.

'I don't have a clue,' he answered indifferently.

'Well, I couldn't find it when I just looked for it, and I know it went into the back of the Range Rover because I saw it go in—a Harrods bag,' she described. 'It has my things in it. If you don't have it, then—' she flung out a hand before folding it back beneath her breasts again '—ring someone and find out what's been done with it.'

Intrigued, despite not wanting to be, Roque went for a dismissive shrug and strode across to his own wall of hanging space, picked a tee shirt at random and pulled it on over his head. 'The staff will have gone off duty by now. It's late. Go to bed. We will find it in the morning.'

'I want my stuff *now*,' Angie stated stubbornly.

'Well, you can't have it now!' he fired back.

He dropped the towel and pulled on a pair of jeans. Angie got a brief glimpse of bronzed muscular flanks, and hated it that certain muscles stung and pulsed.

Without another word she turned and walked away again, back around the bed and into her own dressing room, where she began an angry, noisy search for the Harrods bag. A few minutes later he arrived in the opening, looking tall, dark and dangerous in jeans and a white tee shirt, with his hair still ruffled and a scowl on his too-handsome face.

Ignoring him, Angie continued with what she was doing.

'Explain why you need the bag,' he invited abruptly.

Rummaging through a drawer, she slammed it shut and opened the next one. 'I want my phone.'

'Leaving me again, Angie?' Roque sighed out. 'Hoping to call a cab? This is not London. Cabs don't turn up in five minutes around here.'

'If I was intending to leave you I would have just gone—walked back to Lisbon if I had to.' Straightening up, she lanced him an icicle glance. 'I can't leave,' she added, moving on to check out the bottom of the wardrobes. 'I have to consider my brother's well-being. I want my phone so I can make you stop telling such big lies to me.'

Roque's attention was truly caught now, and this time his frown was not angry but confused. 'I do not understand.'

'I know you don't.'

She found the bag then, hidden behind a pair of long black winter boots, and bent to snatch it up. Crossing to the wall-to-wall dressing table, she tipped the contents out onto the top, found her mobile phone, and started hitting buttons as she walked over to where he stood.

'Listen,' she said, handing the phone to him, and then stood waiting for him to do as she'd said. She didn't look at his face. She didn't care what he was thinking or feeling or—anything. She just waited, with her lips sucked in at the corners to stop them from trembling, knowing exactly what he was listening to.

Nadia herself, confirming the truth about that night twelve months ago. Nadia taunting Angie with it via voicemail, describing all the other nights she and Roque had spent together while Angie had been out of the way.

She knew without looking up at him when the message had finished. She waited, without allowing herself the relief of swallowing the thick lump that had formed in her throat, for him to lower the phone from his ear.

'I saved it as evidence,' she told him. 'In case I decided I could take the humiliation of letting my lawyers listen to it for use in evidence for our div— If you're deleting it,' she broke off to say, when his fingers started hitting buttons, 'then I should tell you I've downloaded a copy elsewhere.'

'Angie—'

'As you said,' she cut right across him. 'We are doing this twelve months too late.'

Snatching the phone back, she turned and walked away from him.

'She is lying, *meu querida*,' he insisted wearily. 'It—none of what she said happened except inside her own twisted head.'

'Well, I don't suppose it matters any more.' She laid the phone down on the heap of other things she'd tipped from the bag. 'If you're telling me the truth then you've just had your payback. If Nadia is telling the truth I suppose I had mine when I kicked you out of my life.'

Wrapping her arms around the jumper, she turned and made herself look at him. He looked—stunned. Maybe even a bit shaken and pale. Crazy, she thought, how seeing him stripped of his usual arrogance made her insides start to shake.

'Now you are back…'

Not liking the way he said that, Angie frowned. She had a feeling he was thinking out loud rather than speaking to her. He even blinked slowly, as if to refocus, and then she watched him take in a short breath.

'You know something, Angie? I think I am ashamed of you,' he said, so unexpectedly that he made her blink. He grimaced and went to turn away, then changed his mind and swung back again. 'I am your husband!' he launched at her. 'Yet you preferred to believe that!' He slashed a contemptuous glance at her mobile. 'The ravings of a mean-minded bad loser out to cause trouble between us, rather than give me the right to defend myself!'

'I saw the newspapers—'

'And received a bitchy message—which, seemingly, you have hugged to yourself like a hair shirt ever since!'

She turned pale, because there was an indefensible slice of truth in that harsh statement. 'Y-you'd already told me you were going to find someone else to take my place. You—'

'And you, *querida*, still made the choice to go to your brother.'

'I ch-changed my mind and came back—'

'*Exatamente,*' Roque said curtly. 'You changed your mind—as was your right… As it was my right to change my mind about putting another woman in your place.'

'Oh, very slick.' Angie utterly derided that. 'I saw you with my own eyes, kissing her!'

'*Sim.*' He revealed absolutely no crack in his superior attitude. 'Guilty as charged. And *you* made it halfway to your brother's school before you decided to turn back.'

The parallel lines he was drawing suddenly dovetailed so neatly Angie almost choked on her breath as the two merged together. He was saying he had taken his threat as far as kissing Nadia before he'd changed his mind.

Her lips trembled and parted. She dropped her arms to her sides. She was hunting her head for a line of defence but could not find one.

As if he knew that, Roque nodded his head, spun a swift final glance of glinting contempt at her mobile, then turned and walked off.

Angie couldn't move a single muscle. The chilly wash of truth was sinking through her as she listened to the suite door open, then shut.

Could he be telling the truth?

She knew she was still hunting for a chink in his cold demolition of her totally self-righteous belief in her own version of what had happened. Face it, Angie, you need to find a chink or Roque is right!

He was certainly right about Nadia's message—she *had* hugged it to her like some self-punishing hair shirt. Her skin was suddenly riddled with a prickly quiver. Spinning round, she snatched up the phone and deleted Nadia's wretched message with tense taps of her finger, then tossed the phone away from her as if it had burned to touch it at all.

She heard the sound of another door closing, and swung around, her breath caught and her eyes glued to the archway, until it registered with her that the door she'd heard closing was the one that led out of the suite.

He'd left her alone to fester. He'd taken his bad temper off to another part of the house. The burning urge to go chasing after him almost got the better of her, but then common sense arrived, telling her to give him time to cool off.

Give them both time to cool off.

It seemed crazily fitting that when she opened the wrong drawer to look for her normal nightdress she found herself staring at a piece of white tissue paper folded carefully over something familiarly soft, with an oh-so neatly scripted label carefully pinned to it.

'My Baby's First Shawl by Angelina de Calvhos' she read with a thick, sinking swoop of her heart. Silly, soppy, sentimental…

As her lips parted and started trembling she felt a different kind of tremor take control of her throat. Reaching out, even her fingers trembled as she slowly, carefully picked up the piece of tissue and placed it gently on the drawer-top. She did not want to look inside it. She had a horrible feeling her heart was going to crack wide open if she did. Yet, with her breath caught in her chest, she still drew back the folds of tissue, then stood, feeling an odd numbness spread up from her toes.

Barely half finished and very amateur-looking, the gossamer-fine snowy white shawl had been her very first attempt at crocheting. She'd spent hours, carefully threading the fine lacy pattern, only to constantly need to unpick half of it again when she realised she'd made a mistake.

Dry-eyed, she saw herself sitting curled up in a chintzy armchair in the tiny cottage deep in the Cotswolds Carla had sent her to when she'd needed to seek refuge from the press.

And from Roque, she added as she stroked her fingers across the soft fine wool. The cottage had belonged to a spinster aunt of Carla's. She'd inherited it when the aunt died, but had rarely used it herself. 'An investment', her boss had called it. For Angie it had become her sanctuary, a place to hide away from the public eye while she nursed her wounds and nurtured the tiny life growing inside her womb. She'd found the hooks, wool and patterns languishing in a cupboard. It had just felt kind of fitting that she occupied some of her time taking on the challenge of teaching herself how to crochet.

'Bad therapy, sweetie,' Carla had drawled in her dry, mocking way, when she'd called in one day and caught her fumbling attempts to work with the hook and wool and demanded to know what she was doing. 'Maternal instincts gone mad. You should come back into the real world before you turn into one of those awful mummy frumps. I've got loads of work for a pregnant model...'

Well, not for *this* model, Angie thought sadly. A week after that conversation with Carla she'd been taken into hospital and confined to complete bedrest in an attempt to stop a threatening miscarriage. A month later it had happened anyway, for no reason anyone could give except the old one about nature taking its course.

Roque had not even known she was pregnant. She had not known it herself until a couple of weeks after their marriage fell apart. She hadn't told her brother. Only Carla knew, and the doctor she'd gone to see. After it was over she'd been glad she'd kept it to herself.

And she had no intention of telling Roque now, she thought as she folded the tiny shawl into its tissue wrapping and placed it back in the drawer. They had enough problems cluttering up their marriage without adding a lost baby to them. What would be gained from telling him now?

What was gone was gone.

Angie slid back into bed and curled up on her side. Closing her eyes, she listened to the steady pump of her own heartbeat and felt as if she was lying in the loneliest place on earth. Roque would not come back into this bed tonight—she just knew that he wouldn't. There was too much angry bitterness bubbling between them, and if he *had* been telling her the truth then...

She caught the sound of a door opening and then closing with a quiet click into its housing. Her heart missed a beat as she lay there, listening to Roque's quiet tread. The whole suite was shrouded in darkness because she'd switched off all the lights before she'd climbed into bed, so she lay listening to the rustle of clothing, then picked up the scent of brandy as he lifted the covers and slid into the bed.

'You are awake,' he said, and it was not a question.

Turning over, she peered at him through the darkness. He was lying on his back, staring up at the ceiling, the covers riding low across his chest. And he looked so very sombre Angie wanted to reach out and stroke her fingers along his unsmiling lips.

'Okay, I have been thinking,' he declared quietly. 'We do not communicate about the right things. This must change.'

Angie thought about that for a couple of seconds, then gave a jerky nod of her head, engrossed in the dark resonance of his accent, which had deepened since they'd stood flinging accusations at each other.

'I should not have brought my—bitterness about what has happened into this bed earlier. My *retribuição* crack was unforgivable in the circumstances, and I apologise for making it.'

'I—'

'Let me finish,' he cut in, and like a naughty child chided for interrupting Angie was silenced. 'The evidence of Nadia has always been stacked against me. I know that. When she lied to the press about our—involvement, I had no way of proving my innocence so I said nothing. That was also a mistake.'

'I sh-should have let you say it, though,' Angie dared to whisper.

'After witnessing that kiss?' He turned his dark head on the pillow and looked at her through the darkness. 'No.' He turned to stare at the ceiling again. 'It was not a kiss a husband should give any other woman but his wife. It should not have happened and you were right to feel cheated. If I had caught you kissing another man like that I would have ripped him limb from limb, then thrown you out of my life without conscience.'

'Not much love lost, then.' Angie could not help throwing in the jibe.

'I am Portuguese,' he claimed, as if it made him different from the rest of the human race. 'We are possessive of our women. We do not forgive infidelity. We don't like to share.'

'If that last bit was aimed at my brother, then I—'

'And your career,' Roque put in. 'Which took you away in one direction while I went off in another... Your brother was an added intrusion I did not...enjoy.'

'Alex was—'

'Your responsibility. And *he* did not like to share.'

'I warned you I would make a lousy wife,' Angie sighed out heavily, flopping onto her back.

'And you were,' he agreed.

'You shouldn't have married me.'

'I was irritated with you as my lover. My arrogance told me I could turn you into a more satisfying wife.'

Angie released a very *un*satisfied breath of air at his note of dry whimsy. It offered no answer at all as to why he'd suggested marriage—or for that matter why she had agreed. Oh, she knew that she'd been wildly in love with him. The 'first love' syndrome had grabbed a really tight hold on her. But they'd been sharing a very exciting and passionate relationship without commitment, so why had he bothered to change the status quo?

Then there was the 'no divorce' thing he'd thrown at her yesterday—or the day before that, she amended, when she remembered the lateness of the hour. What kind of man with a 'no divorce' clause built into his family pride married a woman because she irritated him as a lover?

'And I was in love with you.' He added the flat appendage as if he'd tapped directly into her thoughts.

Angie just froze as a trail of words like, *amo-te*, *eu te amo*, *eu quero te*, echoed in her head. Soul-melting endearments from a handsome ex-playboy, a guy with a fatal charm built into his genes. And she had responded to his softly spoken words with her own English versions… Yet how was it that she'd known absolutely how much *she'd* meant them while not taking on board the true worth of his words?

Then she remembered how those soul-melting endearments had gone missing within a few days of his ring sliding onto her finger, and Angie knew deep inside that she had been the one to blame. She'd continued on in her busy life with blind disregard to the fact that their relationship had changed, or that she needed to make changes along with it. Her wake-up call had arrived too late, when she'd found out she was pregnant two weeks after their marriage had blown apart.

Her eyes began to sting in the darkness as she thought about it. The horrible bad timing, the terrible hurt, the miserable weeks of loneliness when she'd hidden herself away to lick her wounds while hugging the news about their baby to herself, as if he'd forfeited the right to care.

'*W-was…?*' she prompted tremulously. 'As—as in you don't feel that way about me any more?'

Watching her through the sultry darkness, Roque saw the glitter of tears in her eyes and wanted his right to retribution back. Where the hell did she get off, daring to ask him that question after the year she had put him through?

'You think I should still love you?' He threw the loaded ball right back into Angie's court.

Pressing her trembling lips together, she gave a shake of her head, and a burning sense of dissatisfaction grabbed hold of his chest muscles, making him want to take hold of her by the shoulders and give her a damn good shake. So what was new there? he asked himself heavily. He could hardly recall a time when she hadn't annoyed him enough to make him want to shake her until she woke up and recognised what they'd had going for them once.

'*A esperança é a última que morre,*' he quoted heavily.

'I don't know what that means,' she whispered through the darkness.

'Then learn my language,' he suggested without remorse. He added a gruff, 'Go to sleep,' and then a sigh when he recognised he was bringing the last twenty hours in a full circle, with a gap between them in their bed as wide as an ocean.

Only this time Angie wasn't playing. 'Okay, so you're angry with me,' she accepted, drawing in a fortifying breath of air. 'I'm sorry I made you wait twelve months to tell me about Nadia. And I wish I wasn't so stubborn and unforgiving—but if you tell me what I must do one more time, Roque, I will—'

He moved without her seeing it coming. One of his arms just stretched out and appeared through the darkness to grab hold of her wrist, and the next thing Angie knew she was being hauled across the gap between them. She landed against his chest in a quiver of gasps and protests. They looked at each other—two deep-diving seconds of looking—and then his other hand arrived at the back of her head and he was pulling her down to receive the full onslaught of his kiss.

She didn't even think of fighting to get away from him this time. Instead she just kissed him back with every last bit of fevered anxiety she felt running rife in her blood. In fact she was so intent on what she was feeding into her kiss that when she felt something cool slide onto her finger she pulled her head back so hard it was a wonder she didn't snap her neck.

She stared dazedly down at him, watched a mocking little smile take control of his mouth. Then she lifted her left hand and stared at the two rings now slotted onto her finger.

She'd forgotten all about the rings again. She'd forgotten that Roque had taken them back. Her eyes were luminous even without the threat of tears as she looked back at his handsome dark face.

'*A esperança é a última que morre,*' he repeated softly, then pressed her back against the pillow and came over her to capture her lips with another hot, ravishing kiss. Angie's hands found his shoulders, and she set light so fast she almost hyperventilated when he snaked back from her to rear up onto his knees.

'What the hell are you wearing?' he ground out incredulously, staring down at the voluminous folds of white muslin.

'Hair shirt,' Angie whispered. 'I didn't think you would come back to this bed tonight.'

He spread back the covers so he could get a better look at the nightdress. After spending long seconds scanning her, from spiralling flame hair splashed against the pillow down to slender pink toes, he let out a lazy laugh. 'You look like Count Dracula's bride! No, don't fire up, Angelina the sacrifice.' He grinned rakishly when she tensed up. 'I like it.' Reaching down, he tugged the muslin all nice and neat around the shape of her body. 'I think it is appropriate attire for a lady about to be ravished on her wedding night.'

'Bit late for that,' Angie said, shaking out a quiver of pleasure when he ran the flat of his hands all the way up her muslin-covered legs to the feminine curve of her slender hips. 'I got to be well and truly ravished long before my wedding night—and I am not in any way, shape or form a *sacrifice*,' she added, in case he thought she was *that* sorry she hadn't let him defend himself twelve months ago.

'Don't spoil the fantasy.' Sending his hands on a further trail of her muslin-wrapped body, he shaped her narrow ribcage, then located the burgeoning fullness of her breasts. 'We will make *this* our new wedding night, and this time—' he paused to view the successful way he had outlined both budding peaks against the fine cloth with his long fingers '—we will follow it up with the honeymoon we did not manage to enjoy the first time around.'

'You—'

'Shut up now, Angie,' he growled, losing all hint of humour as he lowered his dark head, claimed one nipple in the heat of his mouth, and sucked hard on it through the muslin.

Angie forgot what she had been going to say as she closed her eyes and arched her back, setting free a helpless cry of pleasure. Her fingers dug into his hair. Her thighs sprang apart.

Roque husked out a very masculine laugh. 'Not very virginal, *meu querida*,' he murmured dryly.

'Shut up.' It was Angie's turn to call a halt to talking.

Roque's answer was the swooping glide of a long-fingered hand down between the hot juncture she'd opened up. He touched her through the muslin and sent her spinning her off into an exotic world she did not come away from for a long, long time.

Afterwards she stared up into the all-consuming darkness enfolding them and hoped—prayed—that in giving him the benefit of the doubt about Nadia she was not making the biggest mistake of her life.

CHAPTER NINE

RESTING her forearms against the rail on the sunny balcony, Angie looked down at the swimming pool situated directly below her, where Roque was currently cutting through the water like a man-eating shark.

The air this early still had a chill to it, and she did not know how he could stand it in the water, but then sharks were cold-blooded, she thought with a smile.

Not that she'd been treated to the cold-blooded, man-eating shark in him over the last three weeks. No, she'd had the very *hot*-blooded *woman*-eating shark. The one that circled her like a hunter and would pounce when she was least expecting it to devour her in a fest of passionate lust.

Lust. She pulled a face at the word, because lust was what they shared on this honeymoon. No mention from either of them since the night they'd arrived here of that other word—*love*.

Watching him cut through the water in a long, bronzed slither of supple male magnificence, she was not in the least bit surprised to feel her lust for him tangle up the sensitive muscles low down inside. Beneath the short slip of a nightdress she was wearing, her thighs shifted against a soft pulsing ache that reminded her just how passionately lustful Roque had been as recently as an hour ago, before he had left her to sleep off the effects while he'd taken himself off to his all-purpose gym before his swim.

Roque possessed vibrant energy enough to drive ten men. He was rarely ever still. If he wasn't dragging her off somewhere to show her Portugal from a proud native's perspective, he was using up some of that excess energy in dealing with his many business interests via the fully equipped office on the ground floor. When that failed to hold his restless interest he hunted her down.

As honeymoons went, theirs had been filled with non-stop passion and occasional quick trips out thrown in as respite. He'd flown them in his helicopter to Porto, then down a long stretch of the Douro River, banked by its famed hills and frilled by tier upon tier of wine terraces. And he'd really impressed her by pointing out how many of those terraced hills belonged to him or came beneath the de Calvhos umbrella. Back in Porto they'd boarded his yacht and spent a few days sailing down to the Algarve. And they'd strolled through the smaller vine terraces right here on this estate, when he'd demonstrated what went into producing a wine as exclusive as the coveted d'Agostinho label, and he'd made her drunk from tasting samples directly from the barrel, then laughed when he'd had to carry her back to his car.

He'd been relaxed and fun—a side to him she had rarely glimpsed the last time they been together. Back then they'd both been so busy, reduced to flying in and out of each other's lives with a speed and frequency that shocked and appalled her when she thought about it now. It was no wonder she'd felt wired up when he was with her and cast adrift when he was not. They'd been more like very intimate strangers, passing briefly in the warm passions of the night, than a real husband and wife. Except...

What they had now was not what she would describe as normal, Angie mused with a small frown. Because they hadn't—not once—taken a trip into Lisbon, or visited any of their old social haunts. No long leisurely meals eaten in Tavares' opulent surroundings, nor lively evenings spent with his friends at Club Lux. They had not gone near his city apartment, or strolled the shops on the Avenida da Liberdade. When she'd specially asked if they could go there he'd frowned and murmured some vague promise that they would discuss it later, then suddenly remembered a rush of calls he had to make.

Not that she wanted to shop till she dropped, or hop back onto Lisbon's social merry-go-round. She didn't. Her life had changed last year when she'd lost Roque and then their baby. Her wants and needs and ideals had changed. Perhaps his had, too. But this new life they were leading, encapsulated in a bubble, sealed off and protected from the life they'd used to live, was not sustainable. They couldn't go on for ever locking the rest of the world out.

Angie's frown deepened as she watched Roque make another looping turn in the pool and then spear back the way he had come. Yesterday Carla had called her with a business proposition that had roused her interest. When she'd told Roque about it over dinner he'd been so uncommunicative about the idea they'd almost had their first fight in three weeks.

She'd pointed out to him that if she was to live permanently here in Portugal then setting up a CGM branch here in Lisbon would be the perfect challenge for her. She'd known that by saying it she had been putting the stamp of permanency on their marriage. She'd also been aware that she was taking a huge step by if not stating it out loud then showing that she was ready to put the Nadia thing aside for good.

Roque had taken that on board, she was sure he had, because his attitude had softened and he'd started firing really impressive and well-informed questions at her about CGM, which had forced her to jump through hoops to answer and to grow quite heated when his opinions differed from hers.

They'd taken the argument to bed with them, and finished it off with a different kind of heat. And now here she was, up out of her bed hours before she normally would be, eager to strike while the idea was hot and convince him to—

Distracted from her thoughts by the familiar sound of his mobile's ringtone floating up from the terrace below her, Angie broke into an appreciative grin as she watched him haul himself out of the pool in a glorious ripple of water-washed muscle bronzed by the morning sun.

Gorgeous, she thought lushly, peering down at him like a sneaky voyeur—because he had no idea she was up here spying on him.

He picked the phone up off a table, then stood dripping water while he indulged in a sharp question and answer session in Portuguese. It had to be business, she decided, watching how, even wearing only a pair of black swimming shorts, he had taken on a whole new persona—the cold-blooded, man-eating shark kind.

Her grin widened.

Then suddenly died into stark frozen shock when the impatient snap of his voice drifted up to her. *'Para Deus causa, Nadia, irá você escuta-me!'*

For God's sake—*Nadia*?

The rest didn't matter; she would not have been able to translate it anyway. Her grasp of Portuguese was still sketchy at best, and—

Roque was still in contact with Nadia.

Angie took a jerky step back from the rail, then just stood in her flimsy, peachy strip of a nightdress, feeling the slow chilling growth of shock rise up from her feet while she listened to the impatient cut of Roque's voice fading as he strode into the house.

Silence folded around her like a huge stifling blanket. She didn't know what to do or to think. One part of her brain was throwing up all kinds of excuses—there had to be more than one Nadia out there, and maybe Nadia meant something else in Portuguese...

Or was Nadia right here in Portugal? Was she ringing Roque to arrange where they were to meet?

Are you crazy, Angie? she asked herself. You *know* that Nadia returned to live in her native Brazil last year, after she'd spilled her kiss and tell to the press, and you *believe* Roque's insistence that it was all just a pack of lies anyway.

'You are awake, *senhora*...'

Eyelashes fluttering, Angie turned to find Maria standing in the open doors which led into the bedroom, holding a breakfast tray in her hands. The little maid sounded surprised to find her out here, because she knew all about Angie's preference for lazing in bed each morning while Roque did his macho thing with the gym and the pool.

'*Sim,*' she replied, without knowing she'd said it. A dizzy sensation was beginning to spin in her head.

'You eat out here in the sun this morning, then?' Maria smiled as she stepped forward to place the tray down on the small table. 'It is such a beautiful day, no?'

'Beautiful,' Angie repeated like a dim echo, and pushed a set of icy cold fingers up to cover her mouth. It was trembling, she noticed, and the inside of her mouth and throat felt like dry sand.

Maria busied herself pouring out Angie's first cup of tea for her. As the fragrant scent of Earl Grey wafted towards her she felt her stomach churn.

Next thing she knew she was reeling around to face the doors, and heading towards them as a swirling clutch of nausea suddenly took hold. In her unsteady rush to get to the bathroom she bumped into a chair and knocked it over.

Maria straightened up with a jolt, then spun to stare at her. 'Oh, *senhora*, you are ill!' She heard the little maid gasp.

Angie forced herself to keep moving. Runway training, she kept telling herself over and over. You can make it to the bathroom before you throw up.

She was halfway across the bedroom when the suite door suddenly flew open, halting her mid-step. Turning her head, she saw Roque standing there, still wearing his swimming shorts with a towel looped around his neck. He was frowning as if he was in a bad temper.

'I have to fly to Paris this afternoon,' he growled out when he saw her.

Was Nadia in Paris?

With a muffled choke, Angie took flight on legs that

felt like fragile spindles. The archway ahead kept swimming in and out. She heard Roque say something sharp, and Maria answer him, and then the little maid's arm arrived around her waist to help support her—she had never felt so grateful for anything in her entire life.

Feeling too tall and gangly, and as weak as a rag doll, she let Maria guide her towards the bathroom. She threw up in the toilet bowl with Maria holding her hair back just as Roque arrived in the doorway. She could hear the concern in his voice as he spoke with Maria, then felt his closeness as he took over from the maid until it was over. His strong hands gently lifted her into his arms.

Angie wanted to fight him. She wanted to tell him to get off her. She wanted to scream at him to get out. But she found she couldn't raise the energy, and the dizzying sickness was already trying to pull her back down again.

Maria was still there. She could hear the two of them talking in low voices, but couldn't understand a word that they said.

Well, what did she expect? She'd married a foreigner. She was living in a foreign country and the language was still foreign to her. It wasn't to Nadia. Nadia's native Brazilian was almost an exact match to Roque's Portuguese. She was dark, like him—exotic, like him, and…

He laid her down on the bed, then stretched out to bring the rumpled sheet fluttering over her. Angie huddled beneath it, so cold she was shivering like mad.

'I'm calling the doctor,' he said harshly.

'Don't you *dare* call a doctor!' Angie shrieked out,

then groaned when it made her head feel as if it was splitting apart.

She flinched when she felt the warmth of Roque's palm on her brow. For some reason it brought her eyes flickering open. He was squatting down beside the bed, so close to her she could see tiny golden-brown shards of concern in his eyes.

'Go away,' she whispered, and squeezed her eyes shut again. She didn't want to look at him. She didn't want to blurt out the question stinging on the tip of her dry, acrid-tasting tongue.

Roque viewed her pinched pallor from the taut position of a man who was recalling the times he had cut it too fine with the use of a condom. He might not have any previous experience with morning sickness to draw upon, but his instincts had been yelling the cause at him from the moment he saw her standing there, looking pale as death, with a hand clamped to her mouth.

What else *could* be wrong with her? Maria had told him the smell of the tea had turned Angie's stomach. The maid insisted she'd been perfectly fine a minute before, enjoying the sunshine on the balcony.

'Angie…'

'No doctor,' she mumbled, completely misreading what he had been about to say.

Roque released a sigh and pressed his tense lips together, in a cowardly way glad of her interruption, because it had given him time to think. Maybe he was wrong. Maybe she had eaten something that had upset her stomach. Maybe she'd caught a bug.

He did not want there to be a baby yet. Angie was only twenty-three years old, and already she had been a mother to her brother for six years of her life. She deserved a break—a chance to learn how to be Angie. And, damn it, *he* wanted to learn more about the real Angie he had been watching slowly blossom from behind her old tough shell now that she'd passed on responsibility for her brother to him.

Was she already thinking what he was thinking? Was that the reason she had told him to go away? Was she hating him already and wishing she hadn't allowed him to coax her back into his life?

Coax? he mocked. Blackmail came closer to the truth. Coercion, intimidation—and don't forget the desire for retribution, he told himself, feeling guilt take a stranglehold on his taut throat.

Angie uncurled from her huddle and made herself sit up in the bed. She was already beginning to feel a bit better now the sickening shock had started to wear off.

'M-may I have a drink of water?' she asked, pushing back the tumbled tangle of hair from her face.

Roque stretched out a hand to pick up the vacuum flask standing on the bedside table, and poured some chilled water into a glass.

'Thanks,' she mumbled as he handed the glass to her, but she kept her eyes lowered as she sipped.

She couldn't look at him. She wished he would just go and—and get dressed, or something. Because she needed to be on her own so she could think. Drawing her knees up to her chin, she clutched the chilled glass in equally chilled fingers, glad her hair had slithered forward again and was hiding her face. *For God's sake, Nadia*, was playing over and over inside her head, alongside old lurid headlines like *'The Playboy and the Two Supermodels…'*

She took another trembling sip of her drink.

Roque continued to squat there, watching her with that brooding dark frown on his too-handsome face and giving the impression that he just didn't know what to do or say next. The air of indecisive helplessness he was emitting just did not suit him, and it niggled Angie because she knew that behind it his brain would be working. Any second now it was going to make the connection between his phone call down on the terrace and the balcony directly above it, and the idea of that happening coiled her sensitive stomach into knots.

'You m-mentioned going to Paris?' she mumbled, attempting to throw him off the scent.

He nodded his dark head. 'I received a call this morning about some business I need to attend to—but that no longer counts.' He waved a long-fingered hand in a gesture of indifference to Paris. 'Have you considered that you might be pregnant?'

It was like a shot to her blindside. Angie's chin shot up, her green eyes standing out like emerald pools of shock against the stark white colour of her pinched, strained face. It was the last thing she'd expected him to say—the *last* thing!

'Of course I'm not pregnant!' she choked out. 'I have not—no way—missed a single pill!'

She was taking the contraceptive pill? Why hadn't he known that? Roque asked himself, and tension grabbed a hold of his chest muscles as he had to control the need to release a sigh of relief.

'What gave you such a c-crazy idea in the first place?' Angie demanded, managing to turn an ever paler shade of white.

'It just came into my head,' he responded rather dryly. 'You don't have to snap at me.'

Oh, yes she did! The idea of another pregnancy would scare her witless. She didn't ever want to go through that heartbreaking trauma again!

'Well, I'm not,' she snapped, reaching out to set the glass aside before her trembling fingers dropped it. 'And if you need a reason why I'm feeling like this, then look to yourself,' she told him waspishly, fighting fear and hurt and a million other scary emotions. 'If you let me have two hours' sleep straight without wanting sex with me I feel like I'm on a winning streak—and don't look at me as if I've just stuck a knife in your ribs!'

As he rose up to his full height, Roque's chin went up, two lines of heat streaking high across his taut cheeks. 'Well, then, perhaps my trip to Paris is well timed,' he countered stiffly. 'It will allow you to sleep as many hours as you like for the next couple of nights.'

Was that where Nadia was waiting for him?

Angie threw herself back down against the bed and rolled over. 'Don't wake me up as you leave,' she flipped out, and shut her eyes tight.

A thunderous silence bounced off the walls while he continued to stand there. Angie felt as if her insides were collapsing. A baby... Didn't they have enough problems without him bringing a baby into the mix?

Tears burned like fire in her eyes, 'Will you just—go away?' she breathed thickly. 'I'm—sleepy.'

'Of course. My apologies,' he offered. 'Excuse me for delaying your much needed rest.'

Angie shivered as that crushingly impassive cool he could pull off with such chilling effect washed over her.

She listened to him striding away and pulled the covers up over her head.

She should just ask him outright about Nadia. She knew she should. She should just get it over with and spit the poisoned woman's name out of her mouth! But she couldn't. She was too scared. What if he admitted that he still had a thing going with Nadia? What if she'd misheard and made a horrible fool of herself? What if he was glad of the excuse she'd just handed him to get out of here and meet up with his on-off love in romantic Paris?

Roque cut himself with his wet razor and ripped out a curse. What kind of husband was he that he couldn't take Angie's lippy backlash when she was feeling unwell?

The arrogant, over-sensitive kind, he thought, as he tried to finish the job in hand without taking any more nicks out of his chin.

And what kind of man was he that he was preparing to leave her at all while she was feeling as she did? He was bigger than this, he told himself grimly as he pulled on the trousers to a steel-grey suit and pushed his arms into a striped shirt. Taking offence because she'd landed the blame on him for feeling ill was juvenile. He should be ashamed of himself.

Well, he wasn't going—not to Paris anyway, he decided as he knotted blue silk at his throat. He had this stuff with Nadia he needed to deal with in Lisbon. He'd been putting off facing it for too long because he had not wanted to risk Angie finding out.

His grim mouth twisted in derision at his uncharacteristic act of cowardice. One day she was going to have to know. And he was going to have to tell her before someone else did it for him.

Shrugging into his jacket, he took a deep breath and walked back into the bedroom with the intention of telling Angie that Paris was off the agenda. Only to pull to a stop when all he could see of her was the fiery top of her head.

The sight held him captive for a few seconds, a ruefully amused smile catching hold of his mouth. The last time he'd found Angie like this had been at their London apartment, when she'd foolishly believed he would leave her to sleep in a different bedroom. The rat in him then had taken the decision to haul her out of her blissful sleep. This time the loving husband in him would leave her sleeping and call her later from Lisbon, to let her know where he was.

He left the room as silently as a thief stealing away from a crime scene.

Angie sat up as the door drew shut. He hadn't even bothered to say goodbye to her.

Hurt clambered all over her insides. She hoped his fancy private plane developed engine trouble and kept him imprisoned on the airport tarmac so he couldn't keep his sleazy assignation. She hoped—

Hearing the throaty sound of a car engine, Angie slithered out of bed and walked over to the window to watch as his red Ferrari flashed up from the side of the house, then sped away down the drive with the sun glinting on its shiny bodywork. He had not been able to get away fast enough. Standing here watching him go, she felt as if he'd driven over her body without noticing in his eagerness to get to his lover.

Tears developed. She blinked them away. The rolling waves of shock and hurt still played with the muscles around her stomach. The name Nadia beat like a drum in her head.

Her mobile phone started ringing somewhere in the dressing room, and she turned in a daze and went to find it.

'Good morning, sweetie.' Carla's light, slightly dry voice greeted her. 'Do we have a deal? Are you ready to stop playing the pampered wife and start working on the Lisbon project?'

Angie blinked a couple of times before 'the Lisbon project' meant something. Trying to get her brain into gear was like crawling through mud.

'I…yes,' she answered, because saying no or that she didn't know would make this conversation just too complicated right now. 'I w-was thinking of researching suitable business premises today,' Angie managed to say, with reasonable intelligence—mainly because it was the truth. She *had* been intending to look for suitable premises. 'Do you have any specific ideas in mind as to what you want?'

'Oh, *you're* supposed to know Lisbon, Angie. I've hardly ever visited the place,' Carla answered with a languid lack of interest. 'Somewhere suitably elegant with the right postcode, I suppose. I don't know. Why don't you ask Roque, since this is his brainchild? All I had to do was agree to the concept.'

Angie's head went back as if Carla had punched her. 'You—you mean *Roque* set this up?' Angie could barely get the words past her thick throat.

'He still hasn't told you?' For once in her languid life, Carla's voice sharpened.

'No,' Angie said abruptly. Not even when they'd discussed it the night before.

'It appears I've let his surprise cat out of the bag, then,' sighed Carla. 'He needed to find something for you to do to keep you happy in Portugal, sweetie. And to tell the truth I didn't want to lose you completely. So I thought, if he's happy to shell out the money why not let him set me up in Lisbon? The exotic dark Latin look is very high-fashion right now. With you at the helm, scouting for new talent, we could even put ourselves a jump ahead of our competitors. And, talking about dark Latin models, now that you and Roque have resolved your differences about what happened a year ago, how would you feel about Nadia joining you in the venture?'

Nadia...? Angie suddenly felt as if she was eating glass. 'Wh-why Nadia?'

'Because she's living in Lisbon, too,' said Carla impatiently. 'Don't tell me you didn't know that either, Angie? This is really very bad of Roque—to still be keeping you in the dark about all of this. I suppose he thought it wasn't important. After all, you must believe he's telling the truth when he insists the whole Nadia thing never happened, or you wouldn't have gone back to him, would you?'

Roque *knew* that Nadia was living in Lisbon?

'No,' Angie breathed indistinctly, 'I wouldn't.'

'Well, then, have a good think about the Nadia thing. She will come in very useful since she speaks the lingo. And, like you, she's at a loose end right now.'

'She—she isn't modelling any more?' Angie tried her best to make the question sound casual.

'I know you can be blind when you want to be, Angie, but you surely have not been so blinkered that you didn't know Nadia has been out of the modelling game since she got pregnant last year? I think the baby is a couple of months old now.'

Angie was beginning to feel sick again. And she felt so cold suddenly that she didn't think she was ever going to warm up again. 'Do…?' She had to stop to swallow the thick lump in her throat. 'Do you have a contact address for her?'

'Sure. Wait a second while I access it…'

Angie waited. Angie waited and didn't breathe, and didn't allow herself to think beyond waiting.

'Here it is. Sounds very elegant. The Palácio de Ribeiro. It's—'

Angie cut the connection and tossed the phone away from her as if it burnt. The Palácio de Ribeiro was Roque's city address. It took him just fifteen minutes to walk from there to his Lisbon office building, and… and…

Nadia was living in Roque's Lisbon apartment.

Nothing could have been more black and white.

No wonder he'd spent three weeks avoiding taking her into Lisbon. He'd been scared she might come face to face with his lover before he'd worked out how he was going to convince Angie to accept his sordid little *ménage à trois*.

And a baby.

His baby?

Angie turned and ran for the bathroom. This time it physically hurt, because she was trying to throw up from an empty stomach. By the time she'd managed to make it back to the bedroom it was all she could do to sink down on the bed, where she sat with her eyes closed because the world was spinning.

It was only when she rested a hand against the

sensitive wall of her stomach, because it was still throb-bing, that a sudden and terrifying thought rushed into her head.

She stared down at the hand. What if Roque was right about—?

No—no, please not that, she thought pitifully. But she was already dragging herself to her feet to go and recover her phone. Her eyes were burning, her fingers trembling, as she flicked through the menu looking for her personal calendar. A minute later she was sinking down on the edge of the bed again, a limp and quivering wreck.

CHAPTER TEN

IT HIT Roque when he was halfway to Lisbon, and he almost caused a major pile-up behind him when he slammed his foot down on the brakes.

'Mãe de Deus,' he bit out.

Angie had overheard his telephone conversation with Nadia.

Cursing in every language he could think of, he checked the traffic, then took his chances, swinging the long luxury car into a sleek U-turn that would send him back the way he had come. Car horns sounded in protest—he barely registered them, or the angry shouts of abuse aimed at him as he accelerated away.

Maria had told him they'd been out on the balcony when Angie became ill. His wife—his unashamedly lazy in the morning wife—had decided to get up earlier than usual, and had been standing right above him when he took Nadia's call.

His jawline fiercely clenched, he tried to remember what he'd said, but could recall hardly a damn word. Not that it mattered. He shook his grim head. He knew that he must have called Nadia by name. Just as he knew that Angie had heard him say it. And hearing him say it had made Angie sick to her stomach. It had made her break apart.

Fingers tightening around the steering wheel, he put his foot down hard on the accelerator.

Entering the master suite as Angie strode out from the dressing room, Maria pulled to a breath-catching standstill.

'You go out, *senhora*?' Maria asked, in a voice laced with disbelief—which was not surprising when the last time she'd seen her Angie had been heaving into the toilet bowl.

Now she was dressed in a breathtakingly elegant white linen dress touched with stylised brushstrokes of emerald-green. The dress skimmed Angie's long slender figure, and had *couture* sewed into every invisible seam. The neckline was square, the bodice cinched into the waist by a shiny green belt, and the skirt skimmed midway down her amazingly long thighs. And the shiny green shoes she was wearing elevated her height by an impossible five inches at least.

'To Sintra,' Angie confirmed. 'Will you ask Antonio to bring the Range Rover around to the front steps for me, please?'

'*Sim*, I will see to it.' The little maid nodded. 'You— wish Antonio to drive you?'

Angie shook her head. 'I will drive myself,' she said, for this was one errand she needed to do on her own. She was going to Sintra to find a chemist, so she could purchase a pregnancy testing kit. And she'd needed to pull on all this supermodel armour just to keep her functioning without falling into shattered little pieces.

Maria continued to hover like an anxious bird, not

at all comfortable with this turn of events. 'If—if you like, I could go to Sintra for you,' she offered eagerly. 'It will be no trouble, and Senhor Roque will be back from Lisbon soon—'

Lisbon? Angie frowned. 'He's gone to Paris, Maria,' she informed the little maid.

'No—no. He is gone to Lisbon,' Maria insisted. 'He said he had business there he must attend to this morning, but he will be back as quickly as he can because— because you are f-feeling unwell.'

So the Paris trip was yet another lie he'd told her…

'Tell Antonio about the car, Maria,' Angie breathed unsteadily.

'*Sim, senhora.*' Too well-trained to argue, the maid dipped a stiff little curtsy and whipped out of the room, leaving Angie alone to field this last hard knock to her fragile composure without a witness to watch her do it.

Somehow—she did not remember how—she found herself standing outside the *quinta*'s front entrance. The sun was shining hotly down from an azure sky. Everything around her looked clear and sharp and picture-postcard-perfect—the greens of the gardens, the bright pinks and purples of the trailing bougainvillaea against the apricot walls of the house, and the shiny black bulk of the Range Rover awaiting her at the bottom of the front steps.

She did not recall climbing into it. She did not recall switching on the engine and driving away. She fixed all her concentration on finding her way to Sintra in a car she had never driven before, on roads as foreign to her as the husband to whom she had given all her faith.

Roque slowed down to take the turn in through the gates of the Quinta d'Agostinho then powered up again to shoot the car into the tunnel of leafy trees. Coming out into the bright sunlight a few minutes later, he saw his home standing sure and solid in its elegant spread of sweeping lawns, backed by a forest of trees.

He glanced up at the balcony situated directly above the swimming pool, envisaged Angie standing there listening to the conversation taking place below her, and felt as if his skin was peeling back from his flesh as he played out what had happened next.

But that weird feeling was nothing compared to the one he experienced when he drove down towards the garages and saw that his Range Rover was missing. Diving out of his car, he strode into the house and shouted for Zetta at the top of his voice. His housekeeper came hurrying into the grand hallway from the rear of the house.

'Where is the Range Rover?' he demanded, a shade unsteadily.

The housekeeper wrung her hands together. 'The *senhora* take it out, Senhor Roque. Maria said she has gone into Sintra.'

Sintra? A wave of relief flooded through him. For a few minutes there he'd convinced himself that Angie had done a runner on him again, and was already on her way to the airport, meaning to disappear off the face of the earth.

'Why has she gone to Sintra?' He frowned, not seeing a link between the reason he had come rushing back here and their local town.

'I do not think Maria asked,' Zetta answered. 'She was more concerned that the *senhora* insisted on driving herself when she has on these very high shoes—'

Roque's tension levels shot up again. 'Are you telling me that Antonio is not driving her?'

Still wringing her hands, Zetta nodded.

'But she does not know the car. She does not know the roads. She hardly ever drives herself anywhere, and—*Mãe de Deus*.' His voice broke down into a low hoarse husk. 'She is—unwell…'

The moment Angie realised that she was completely and utterly lost came around two hours later. Pulling the car onto a clearing somewhere way up in the hills, overlooking the sea, she sat back with a sigh of defeat.

She'd found her way into Sintra by following the well-posted road signs. She'd even found a convenient car park, and her purchase now lay with her bag on the seat next to her. Everything up to that point had been so much easier than she'd expected it to be—but she'd soon learned that getting back to the Quinta d'Agostinho was a different matter altogether.

Roque's private estate was not signposted. And the road out of Sintra had taken her a different way from the one on which she'd come in. It had seemed logical that so long as she kept on driving she would eventually notice something familiar to use as a guide.

'Great logic, Angie,' she mumbled.

Now the sun was high, and the car was already stifling. She'd only killed the air-conditioning two minutes ago, when she'd switched off the car engine.

Reaching up, she ran a hand around the back of her neck and lifted her hair away from her hot skin. On the seat beside her with her bag was the half-drunk bottle of water she'd had the sense to purchase before she got herself lost. And beside it lay her mobile phone, which she'd tried to use several times only to discover there was no signal. On an act of pure frustration she'd switched the stupid thing off.

Still… With little hope that it was going to be any different this time, she let her hair fall back down onto her nape, then reached for the phone and switched it on again.

The moment it had powered up the messages began downloading like flickering shouts. Most of them from Roque, she saw. A couple from Carla, and even one from her brother, who had been calling her twice a week since he'd gone to Brazil—duty calls, to reassure her that he was enjoying himself, Angie recognised with a grimace of a smile.

About to try calling Roque again, she felt the phone suddenly leap into life in her fingers.

'Angie? *Graças a Deus*. Where the hell are you?' Roque's deep rasping voice raked into her ear.

'Lost,' she admitted. 'Up in the hills somewhere.'

'Lost? In the hills?' he repeated, as if most of Portugal wasn't covered in them. 'Why didn't you call to tell me so?'

'No signal until now,' she explained, feeling oddly as if she was having this conversation with a complete stranger rather than the husband she'd discovered was a lying cheat.

A stunning silence fell down between them for several seconds, then she heard Roque pull in a deep breath. 'Okay, so you are lost,' he murmured more calmly. 'Be a good girl and activate the car's satellite navigation system. It will pinpoint your position and then you can tell me what it says. I will come and get you.'

'But I don't want you to come and get me,' Angie told him.

'Yes, you do!' Roque exploded all over again. 'Have you any idea how much trouble you've caused by getting lost? Maria is weeping all over the place, and I was about half a minute away from calling the police. Only a madwoman drives off into the hills without knowing where she is going, so do as I tell you, Angie, and switch on the damn—'

The line went dead. Roque bit out a string of filthy curses. Lost in the hills… He turned full circle, a set of long fingers scoring through his already dishevelled hair, then grabbed hold of the back of his neck. She'd been gone for hours, so she could be anywhere.

When did he get to be so stupid? How did *she* get to drive at all in the kind of shoes Maria had described?

He tried to connect to her phone again.

Angie ignored the phone's ring while she touched buttons until she finally brought the satellite navigation screen to life, then she sat staring at the screen. It showed her a map with hardly anything on it except for a thin thread of road. All the information was in Portuguese. With no clue as to how she changed it to English, or even if she could change it, the map was, therefore, of absolutely no use.

She recovered her phone and allowed the connection. 'I've got the satellite thing working, but—'

'Angelina, I am about to lose my temper here.' Roque's grim voice cut across hers. 'So do yourself a favour and don't cut our connection again!'

'It's all in Portuguese,' she continued as if he had not interrupted her. 'You are going to have to tell me what to do so that I can understand it.'

She heard him suck in another deep breath. She felt him fighting to control his temper. Angie did not offer up any encouragement, just waited until he spoke again. 'I will talk you through it, so concentrate...'

The drive back down through the forest-strewn hills was relatively simple now she had her own personal pilot to guide her, Angie discovered. Roque had instructed her on how to make the car's computer recognise her mobile phone, and now the deep cool sound of his voice filled the car via its speakers, firing questions and directions at her as she drove. In a strange way Angie found it comforting to have him there with her, though she wasn't sure why—because she had certainly shut down from *feeling* anything else right now.

Self-preservation kicking in, she assumed, as she glimpsed signs of civilisation appearing in front of her, and only a few minutes later she was joining the main highway. Relief was a feeling, she acknowledged as she heaved out another sigh.

It was only a short second later that a red Ferrari flashed up beside her, then shot past, only to pull in front of her two metres away from her front bumper.

'Is that you?' she gasped in surprise.

'*Sim*, it is me,' Roque responded.

'But—what are you doing here?'

'I am here to make sure that you don't get lost again before I have had a chance to throttle you, *meu querida*,' he explained, so smoothly Angie almost missed the threat threading through his silken tone.

'Just—go to hell, *meu querido*,' Angie said, and switched the phone off, preferring to finish the rest of the journey following his car without having to listen to him at the same time.

She hated him, she remembered. He was a lying, cheating, self-seeking playboy. The minute she got back to the house she was going to pack her things and *leave*. Her head was aching. She hadn't eaten anything all day. She had a stupid pregnancy test lying on the seat beside her, and *he* had his mistress waiting for him not far away.

The first strangled sob tore from her as she followed him through the *quinta* gates, then into the tunnel of trees. By the time she came out again into hot bright sunlight the tears were trickling down her cheeks.

She stopped the car behind his at the front steps, then reached up to wipe the tears away with one hand while the other fumbled to unlock her seat belt. Reaching for her things from the seat beside her, she was about to open the car door when it suddenly flew open, and Roque stood there, looking less than his usual immaculate self.

Angie allowed herself a brief flickering glance at him. His hard-edged face was marblelike, the golden skin across the curving sweep of his cheekbones pulled tight. He stuck out a long-fingered hand in a grimly silent offer to assist her to alight from the car, but she ignored it, preferring to slide her long legs out over the high sill to land on slender heels the length of five-inch spikes.

The hand stretched out again, as if to steady her just in case the slender heels would not support her, and Angie quivered. 'Don't touch me,' she whispered, then brushed around him and ran up the steps to the house.

Ramming his rejected hand into a fist, Roque watched her almost twist off one of the ridiculous shoes in her rush to get away from him, and bit back a colourful oath. 'For God's sake, Angie, be careful—'

For God's sake, Angie turned into *For God's sake, Nadia* in her head, and her spine shot erect with a jerk as she strode as fast as she dared into the house

She'd already crossed the vast empty space of the grand hallway and was running up the stairs by the time Roque reached the front door. Her white and green dress clung to every slender curve and her hair hung in a rich river of fire between her taut shoulderblades. The shoes were too high. The marble staircase was unforgiving to anyone who should fall on it. He'd seen the tracks of tears streaking her pale cheeks before she'd pushed past him, and—

'Slow down before you break your neck!' he roared as he strode after her. 'You are *not* going to shake me off, Angie, so you might as well stop trying!'

Angie had reached the graceful curve of the upper landing by then, and she spun round and leant over the banister. Halfway up the marble staircase Roque paused and looked at her, and that unfair, totally unyielding crash of attraction she always felt when she looked at him caught Angie full-on. The way he was standing there, with one foot elevated to the higher step, one long-fingered hand resting lightly against the banister rail sensually—as if he was caressing the rich dark colonial wood. Everything about him was sensual, from the untidy state of his jet silk hair to the striped shirt hanging open at his throat. The unsmiling taut mouth, the slightly flaring nostrils, the deep, dark bottomless eyes looking at her with...

'You are a total womanising rat.' She broke down on the first helpless sob. 'If—if I had a knife handy I would be jumping over this rail so I could plunge it into your chest!'

Roque released a sigh. 'I can explain about Nadia—'

'Don't you *dare* use that woman's name in front of me!' she choked out. 'I don't know why you didn't marry *her*, since you obviously can't live without h-her.'

'What you overheard on the terrace this morning was—'

'Do I look as if want an explanation?' Angie tossed down at him like an electric thunderbolt. 'And anyway, it's too late. I *know* all about Nadia and her baby. I *know* you have them neatly stashed away inside your stupid Lisbon apartment.'

His expression changed. She saw the guilty flicker. 'Angie—'

'Don't you dare come up here,' she said as he started walking again. 'If you come up here I will kill you, I promise. I don't want you near me ever again!'

And with that she leapt away from the rail and ran to shut herself in their suite. She wanted to throw herself down on the bed and sob her eyes out, but knowing he could only be a few seconds behind her she locked herself inside her bathroom instead.

When she came out again she was wrapped in her bathrobe, having spent ages just standing beneath the fierce shower jets, pale as milk. The need to shed tears all over the place had gone now. In fact she felt horribly hollow and flat.

There was no sign of Roque, though she did not go looking around the rest of the suite to check. Instead she walked over to the centre island unit, slid open one of the drawers, then lifted out the tissue-wrapped parcel and laid it down gently on the top.

Perhaps it was fated that Roque should approach her right then, with the silent stealth of a mugger. The first Angie knew of his presence was when his hands came from behind her and settled on the top of the unit, effectively trapping her within the circle of his body and his arms. He'd showered too, she noticed as she picked up on the clean scent of his soap. And he was wearing a matching bathrobe to the one she was wearing.

'Let us get a few things straight while we have some calmness here,' he murmured, bringing his dark head low enough that his breath brushed her cheek. 'Nadia is *not* my mistress.'

With her head dipped, Angie responded with an inelegant sniff.

'Her baby is not *my* baby. She does *not* live in my apartment. She lives in the one *below*, with the man she *married* several months ago. *He* is her baby's father. He is Brazilian, very rich, quite old, and just out of a nasty divorce in Rio in which Nadia was cited as the adulterous cause—hence their swift move here, away from the hostile backlash.'

Angie hunched her shoulders inside the white towelling and said not a word.

Roque inhaled a deep breath. 'I know I should have told you about Nadia before now,' he continued. 'But I am stupid and arrogant. And three weeks ago I wanted to keep Nadia as a weapon to use against you if you—if you hurt me again. Also, I did not see why I should be forced into defending myself for something I did not do. Since then there has not seemed to be the right moment for me to tell you she is here in Lisbon, so I kept the information to myself—like a coward.'

When Angie still held her silence, even with the deliberate provocation he'd offered her with the coward confession, he invited, 'Will you say something? Even if it is only *I hate you, Roque…*'

'I'm pregnant,' Angie whispered.

For a few wretched seconds she thought he hadn't understood her, because he remained so silent and still.

So she tried again. 'I said I am pregnant.'

'I heard you,' he husked.

'I w-went to Sintra to buy a testing kit, and I am positively, properly p-pregnant…again.'

The last word came out all wobbly. She tried swallowing and found she couldn't. She tried blinking the moisture out of her eyes but it just swam back in. Behind her she could feel the throbbing power of his tension. Lifting her hands off the white tissue, she closed them into fists.

'Explain the *again* part,' he said finally.

Angie tried again to swallow the trembling lump in her throat, then just let it all pour out. He did not move a single muscle. He wasn't even breathing as far as she could tell. When she faltered to a halt, the final thing to tremble from her lips was, 'Now I'm scared the same thing is going to happen again…'

Trying to drag himself out of the dark place his mind had gone into, Roque blinked his eyes. The one small chink of light he could see in what she had just confessed to him was that at least this time she was standing here telling him, instead of running away to hide.

And she had every right to feel scared. *He* felt scared. And the same damn issues that had torn their marriage apart twelve months ago were still hanging around, threatening to do the same thing again.

'I bought the apartment from Nadia's husband this morning. They have decided to move to Spain.' he said, not surprised when Angie quivered in front of him. He'd hurt her by ignoring the import of what she'd said. But he was not ignoring it. He was cleaning it. 'When I explained to him the predicament I was in due to our past dealings with Nadia he was not pleased. He had no idea that she'd done to another marriage what she had done to his own. The difference for him is that he *did* have an affair with her. She *did* conceive his child—his only child. His son. And…' His voice wavered ruefully. 'He loves her. I saw the evidence in his face because I *know* how it feels to love someone so badly you are stuck with that one true love for life.'

'*Badly?*' Angie squeezed out.

'As in bad for me,' Roque confirmed. 'I did not want your brother nudging in between us. I did not want your career commitments to take precedence over mine. That kiss with Nadia on the dance floor was me behaving badly. When the result of it blew up in my face and you walked away from me I got what I deserved. I gave you nothing but hassle and heartache.'

'No…' At last Angie stopped just standing there, still hiding from him, and swivelled round to wrap her arms tightly around his waist. 'I was a lousy wife to you. I *let* Alex nudge in between us. I *drove* you into Nadia's arms. I was wildly in love with you but didn't know how to love you. I'm so sorry,' she finished helplessly. 'I should have told you about—about the baby. You had a right to know. Instead I hid away.'

'Because I let you down.'

Angie shook her head. 'I let *you* down. I sh-should have given you the opportunity to explain about Nadia.'

'I let you down,' he repeated grimly. 'I let you down because I was not there when you needed me more than you had ever needed me. I think that makes me a lousy husband, Angie. If you want to stick that knife in my chest I will let you.'

He was not joking. 'I think I've already done it,' Angie murmured contritely.

'*Sim,*' Roque agreed. 'Now you say you are pregnant again.'

'And I'm scared,' she repeated, in case he had missed that bit when she'd said it earlier.

He hadn't. Without the slightest of warning he gathered her up into his arms and carried her through to the bedroom. Dragging back the covers, he deposited her on the bed, then came down beside her and enclosed her in his embrace.

'You are going to stop thinking about the worst-case scenario, okay?' he instructed.

'Okay.' Angie nodded.

'Let me do all the worrying for you.' He lifted a hand to stroke her hair away from the side of her face. 'You just think pleasant thoughts from now on, and we will deal with this together—as we should have done the time before.'

Angie nodded again.

'No more running around in high-heeled shoes. No more getting lost in hills. And no more fights about stupid Nadia,' he added. 'In fact, no more fights at all.'

'Okay,' Angie agreed.

'First thing we do tomorrow is go and see a doctor. If necessary we will fly over to London and consult with a—'

'I hope you feed me before then,' Angie posed wistfully. 'I haven't eaten a thing today and I'm starving to death.'

'Why didn't you say so before?' He was already trying to get up when Angie grabbed hold of him and brought him back to her.

'No, don't go,' she breathed tautly. 'I like it when you hold me. It makes me feel—safe.'

'Loved,' Roque said with a faint edge of tension as he came back into her embrace. 'The word you hesitated over using is *loved*.'

'Loved and safe, then,' Angie extended, then her beautiful green eyes misted over and her soft mouth trembled. 'I love you so much,' she whispered softly. 'I was so miserable when I thought I'd lost you.'

That edge of tension left him, and he gathered her closer so he could cover her mouth with a slow, incredibly tender kiss.

Of course the kiss didn't stay slow and tender. It never could for them. As the passion intensified and their legs tangled together and their breathing quickened, Angie was not in the least bit amused when he suddenly drew back.

'We can't,' he groaned out hoarsely, flinging himself flat onto his back. 'We have to think about the baby now.'

He was oh-so right, and Angie just didn't know what so say. Sorry seemed appropriate, because she just couldn't imagine how they were going to manage for long months without indulging their desire for each other—if she carried this baby through to the end.

'I could always...' She fed a hand down his long tense body, only to have Roque snatch it away.

'I wasn't complaining,' he said frowningly. 'Don't even think like that again.'

'Sorry,' whispered from her lips in genuine contrition. 'I was being—impulsive.'

'You were being adorable,' he groaned, rolling over to gather her in close again. 'We will just have to practise self-control, that's all.'

'Or...we could get up and drive into Lisbon to see the doctor now. Check out what's safe for us and what isn't?'

Eyes like black caverns spun with hints of bronzed mockery captured hers. 'You insatiable witch,' Roque murmured.

Angie just looked up at him and said nothing. He shifted his gaze to her defiantly pouting mouth. A lazy teasing smile spread across his own mouth, then suddenly died again.

'Okay, let's go,' he announced.

The water was glorious, all warm and silkily soapy. Angie lay in it, feeling like an exotic siren being pampered by her loving slave.

'If this bump grows any bigger we will have to install a deeper bath,' Roque complained as he stroked the flat of his hand over her tightly swollen abdomen.

'You love this bump,' Angie murmured lazily. 'You love getting into this bath with me.'

Water sloshed as he shifted his position and came to stretch out at her side, his long, lean bronze-skinned body the perfect contrast to Angie's pearly white slenderness—not including the bump.

'It works for us, my voluptuous one,' he teased her, stroking his fingers around the soapy globe of one lush breast. 'When I am ready, I can slide inside you with the minimum of effort required on your part—and don't you just love it when I do?'

The roaming hand slid lower, meandering away from her breast so he could replace his fingers there with his mouth. Angie stirred on a sensuous murmur of pleasure. The roaming fingers dipped between her thighs, sending her eyelashes fluttering upwards and her head turning on its waterproof pillow.

'Kiss me,' she begged.

Her handsome slave complied. Her arms lifted up, then fell again around his neck, and he made the kiss mimic the sensuous action of his caressing fingers.

It was all so gloriously beautiful she murmured, 'Love you,' against his lips.

'Show me,' he encouraged, and she did show him. She wasn't so restricted by her advanced pregnancy that she could not indulge him as much as he was indulging her.

The first few months had meant weeks of restraint and carefully controlled anxiety, until she'd finally accepted that she was not going to miscarry this precious baby as she had their first child. These last few months had been filled with the most wonderful moments of pure happiness and exquisite lovemaking, with days filled with planning for their baby, and nights filled with perfect passion offered by the man who loved her more than she'd ever dared believe was possible.

She loved to feel his senses quicken for her. She loved

to see the burning heat of his desire for her blaze in his eyes. She loved it when he came over her, as he was doing now, and made that first slow drive with his hips that joined them. She loved to see the fierce depth of his desire for her strip everything but his love for her from his beautiful face.

Reaching up, she touched his lips with her fingers, and smiled tenderly when he kissed them. Then she wasn't smiling—she was drowning, in him, and in what he could make her feel.

Later they lay together in their bed, with the winter moonlight tracing a path across the windows. Angie felt her baby give her a pummelling kick, and smiled when Roque soothed his son with a stroke of his hand.

'To think,' she said, 'we almost lost all of this.'

It didn't seem possible they had come so close to the brink.

'*A esperança é a última que morre,*' Roque murmured.

'You've said that before.' Angie turned to look at him. 'What does it mean?'

One of those impassive smiles she found difficult to read passed across his face. 'Hope is the last one to die,' he translated.

He had never lost faith.

'Oh, Roque, come and look at this,' Angie called softly.

She was leaning on their balcony rail, looking down on the pool terrace below. Feeling the stroke of his hands as they claimed her waist, Angie indicated with her head to the sunny terrace, where her brother Alex sat on a sun lounger with their son sitting within the protective circle of his strong tanned legs.

Alex was reading out loud from one of his course books, while six-month old Luis listened, his attention fixed on his uncle's face and the melodious resonance of his voice.

'Do you think we have produced a genius?' Roque posed dryly.

'They get on like a house on fire.' Angie smiled. 'My handsome grown-up brother and my beautiful son.'

'I am feeling left out again,' her handsome husband murmured.

'Oh, dear.' She turned around to look at him. 'Three—I have *three* demanding men to deal with,' she sighed.

'And you love it.' Roque had no sympathy. 'Your beautiful son had you to himself all morning. Your handsome brother had you to himself all afternoon. When is it my turn?'

As if he did not know, thought Angie, as she laughed and allowed him to draw her in through the balcony doors.

Angie sent him a questioning look when he stepped around her to pull the doors shut. 'I am saving your blushes because you are about to get noisy,' he explained.

Angie blushed anyway. 'You are—'

'Mad for you,' Roque inserted, silencing her with his first scorching kiss.

Coming Next Month

from **Harlequin Presents® EXTRA.** Available July 12, 2011

#157 A SPANISH AWAKENING
Kim Lawrence
One Night in...

#158 RECKLESS NIGHT IN RIO
Jennie Lucas
One Night in...

#159 THE END OF FAKING IT
Natalie Anderson
His Very Personal Assistant

#160 HER NOT-SO-SECRET DIARY
Anne Oliver
His Very Personal Assistant

Coming Next Month

from **Harlequin Presents®.** Available July 26, 2011

#3005 THE MARRIAGE BETRAYAL
Lynne Graham
The Volakis Vow

#3006 THE DISGRACED PLAYBOY
Caitlin Crews
The Notorious Wolfes

#3007 A DARK SICILIAN SECRET
Jane Porter

#3008 THE MATCHMAKER BRIDE
Kate Hewitt
The Powerful and the Pure

#3009 THE UNTAMED ARGENTINEAN
Susan Stephens

#3010 PRINCE OF SCANDAL
Annie West

Visit www.HarlequinInsideRomance.com
for more information on upcoming titles!

HPCNM0711

REQUEST YOUR FREE BOOKS!

2 FREE NOVELS PLUS
2 FREE GIFTS!

YES! Please send me 2 FREE Harlequin Presents® novels and my 2 FREE gifts (gifts are worth about $10). After receiving them, if I don't wish to receive any more books, I can return the shipping statement marked "cancel." If I don't cancel, I will receive 6 brand-new novels every month and be billed just $4.05 per book in the U.S. or $4.74 per book in Canada. That's a saving of at least 15% off the cover price! It's quite a bargain! Shipping and handling is just 50¢ per book in the U.S. and 75¢ per book in Canada.* I understand that accepting the 2 free books and gifts places me under no obligation to buy anything. I can always return a shipment and cancel at any time. Even if I never buy another book, the two free books and gifts are mine to keep forever.

106/306 HDN FC55

Name	(PLEASE PRINT)

Address	Apt. #

City	State/Prov.	Zip/Postal Code

Signature (if under 18, a parent or guardian must sign)

Mail to the **Reader Service:**
IN U.S.A.: P.O. Box 1867, Buffalo, NY 14240-1867
IN CANADA: P.O. Box 609, Fort Erie, Ontario L2A 5X3

Not valid for current subscribers to Harlequin Presents books.

**Are you a current subscriber to Harlequin Presents books
and want to receive the larger-print edition?
Call 1-800-873-8635 or visit www.ReaderService.com.**

* Terms and prices subject to change without notice. Prices do not include applicable taxes. Sales tax applicable in N.Y. Canadian residents will be charged applicable taxes. Offer not valid in Quebec. This offer is limited to one order per household. All orders subject to credit approval. Credit or debit balances in a customer's account(s) may be offset by any other outstanding balance owed by or to the customer. Please allow 4 to 6 weeks for delivery. Offer available while quantities last.

Your Privacy—The Reader Service is committed to protecting your privacy. Our Privacy Policy is available online at www.ReaderService.com or upon request from the Reader Service.

We make a portion of our mailing list available to reputable third parties that offer products we believe may interest you. If you prefer that we not exchange your name with third parties, or if you wish to clarify or modify your communication preferences, please visit us at www.ReaderService.com/consumerchoice or write to us at Reader Service Preference Service, P.O. Box 9062, Buffalo, NY 14269. Include your complete name and address.

HP11

*Once bitten, twice shy. That's Gabby Wade's motto—
especially when it comes to Adamson men.
And the moment she meets Jon Adamson her theory
is confirmed. But with each encounter a little something
sparks between them, making her wonder if she's been
too hasty to dismiss this one!*

*Enjoy this sneak peek from ONE GOOD REASON
by Sarah Mayberry, available August 2011
from Harlequin® Superromance®.*

Gabby Wade's heartbeat thumped in her ears as she marched to her office. She wanted to pretend it was because of her brisk pace returning from the file room, but she wasn't that good a liar.

Her heart was beating like a tom-tom because Jon Adamson had touched her. In a very male, very possessive way. She could still feel the heat of his big hand burning through the seat of her khakis as he'd steadied her on the ladder.

It had taken every ounce of self-control to tell him to unhand her. What she'd really wanted was to grab him by his shirt and, well, explore all those urges his touch had instantly brought to life.

While she might not like him, she was wise enough to understand that it wasn't always about liking the other person. Sometimes it was about pure animal attraction.

Refusing to think about it, she turned to work. When she'd typed in the wrong figures three times, Gabby admitted she was too tired and too distracted. Time to call it a day.

As she was leaving, she spied Jon at his workbench in the shop. His head was propped on his hand as he studied blueprints. It wasn't until she got closer that she saw his eyes were shut.

He looked oddly boyish. There was something innocent and unguarded in his expression. She felt a weakening in her resistance to him.

"Jon." She put her hand on his shoulder, intending to shake him awake. Instead, it rested there like a caress.

His eyes snapped open.

"You were asleep."

"No, I was, uh, visualizing something on this design." He gestured to the blueprint in front of him then rubbed his eyes.

That gesture dealt a bigger blow to her resistance. She realized it wasn't only animal attraction pulling them together. She took a step backward as if to get away from the knowledge.

She cleared her throat. "I'm heading off now."

He gave her a smile, and she could see his exhaustion.

"Yeah, I should, too." He stood and stretched. The hem of his T-shirt rose as he arched his back and she caught a flash of hard male belly. She looked away, but it was too late. Her mind had committed the image to permanent memory.

And suddenly she knew, for good or bad, she'd never look at Jon the same way again.

Find out what happens next in ONE GOOD REASON, available August 2011 from Harlequin® Superromance®!

Celebrating

Blaze **10** *years of*

red-hot reads

Featuring a special August author lineup of
six fan-favorite authors who have written
for Blaze™ from the beginning!

The Original Sexy Six:

Vicki Lewis Thompson
Tori Carrington
Kimberly Raye
Debbi Rawlins
Julie Leto
Jo Leigh

Pick up all six Blaze™
Special Collectors' Edition titles!

August 2011

Plus visit
HarlequinInsideRomance.com
and click on the Series Excitement Tab
for exclusive Blaze™ 10th Anniversary content!

www.Harlequin.com